Gideon Ahoy!

William Mayne

Gideon Ahoy!

Delacorte Press

Published by
Delacorte Press
Bantam Doubleday Dell Publishing Group, Inc.
666 Fifth Avenue
New York, New York 10103

This edition was first published in Great Britain by
Viking Kestrel.

Library of Congress Cataloging in Publication Data

Mayne, William, 1928–
    Gideon ahoy! / by William Mayne.
        p.   cm.
    Summary: Twelve-year-old Eva's chaotic but cheerful
family life in a small English town changes when Gideon,
her brain-damaged deaf older brother, gets a job opening
bridges and locks for the local canalboat.
    ISBN 0-440-50126-1
    [1. Brain-damaged children—Fiction.   2. Deaf—
Fiction.   3. Handicapped—Fiction.   4. Family life—
Fiction.   5. Canals—Fiction.   6. England—Fiction.]
I. Title.
PZ7.M4736Gi   1989
[Fic]—dc19   88-21830
                                                              CIP
                                                              AC

Manufactured in the United States of America

March 1989

10   9   8   7   6   5   4   3   2   1
BG

*For SIMON, who does not understand the words
themselves, but knows why they are here*

CHAPTER ONE

Somewhere an aeroplane.

Gideon waking in the next room with a shout, his morning shout.

He can't tell he does that, thought Eva, coming out of sleep herself, in the next room, opening a silent eye. Does that, she wondered, make a great noise for someone? Am I deaf to light like Gideon is deaf to sound?

Gideon getting out of bed with a thump on the floor.

Eva opened another eye. Daylight in them both, there was, and daytime too.

It's not getting in, she thought; I'm all right in here without it.

Gideon bellowing for Mummy. It was his whisper to the world. It was no use calling back to him. Mum called

7

to him, however, but that would be part of her seeing him, him seeing her.

Gideon giving a glad good-morning howl to Mum, and then going off down the stairs making a buzzing noise. Eva knew he would be holding his head to one side because of the noise in it. He was not deaf to that.

Gideon downstairs in the kitchen, banging the kettle on the tap. Mum getting up and following him down.

Eva let the daylight fall from her eyes, and there was a comfortable space inside, black to her toes, black to her fingers, soft in her mind. Her mind had a memory of Gideon very young, before he was deaf, before he was ill, when he talked clearly and heard perfectly, understood what he saw and heard.

Eva opened her eyes again. The thought had not been a memory at all, but belonged to a time before she was born. Being now twelve she could not recall things that happened when Gideon was not quite three, fifteen years ago. But she knew exactly how Gideon would have been then.

And I can prove it, she thought. The proof came from the fourth bedroom, where Tansy and Mercury were asleep and awake: one was waking the other, Mercury his sister or Tansy her brother.

Eva sat up, looked at her clock, saw it was seven, and got up. For Gideon all times of the day were the same, particularly when he was hungry. It was all Now to him. He had no system for time. Tansy and Mercury had very undeveloped systems, and the result was the same. Eva had a system that said Now was about to begin, but not just yet, please, so there was no need to worry about it. Time was all Then for her.

Next door Tansy and Mercury began to kill each other, which always sounded as if it would happen Now, but never had, and probably wouldn't Then. They became quiet, both dead or both finding something else to do.

Outside, the green hillside was quiet itself, but noisy with birds. Drops of resting rain fell from the leaves of little trees and the growing ends of woodbine and ivy. The sun shone down along the leaves and seemed to make something hot, where a small mist rose.

These days there was a wilderness, called Edenfields, where there was once a brickyard, clay and kilns and business. Now there were buried bricks, and one chimney over an abandoned brick-hearth.

Only Grandpa Catt now searched for sound bricks.

An animal, not Grandpa, walked in the undergrowth across the hill, leaving a darker shaken track behind it where drops of water ran down. A little wind turned leaves and they rustled, large drops falling out of them, the leaves lifting higher afterwards.

Eva went downstairs and out of the door. The sun smashed into her, coming up the valley from the east. Down by the river, in a little boat-yard, someone began to hammer. On the canal, a little nearer and higher up, where the water lay without movement, a duck was gargling, sitting perfectly in the middle of a set of ringed ripples. Further along a pointed ripple swam to the other side, climbed out of the water, shook itself, and walked away under the grasses.

Next door the fowls in the enclosure stalked about, groaning happily, writing in the dust with a claw and correcting with a sudden beak.

Eva remembered what the day was, what it was to be, what Then had been arranged for it.

She went in to see what Gideon thought about it: it was to be his day, not hers. But Gideon thought that words like Tomorrow and Soon and Yesterday and Perhaps were all a variety of No. For him there was now or never.

Yet, like a dog, he sensed something was different in this Now. He was sitting in the kitchen with a different lift to his eyes and shoulders, eating toast and butter and drinking tea, stirring it vigorously and over.

'He likes toast,' said Mum. 'It gives him a crunch too. We want to learn to talk toast.'

'Dththth,' said Gideon. If you knew him you understood that he meant, 'Good morning Eva, I am pleased to see you. Would you like some toast. Mummy will get me some more toast now, I know.'

It was so clear that Eva said, 'Yes please,' and Gideon pushed the butter in her direction.

'We know,' said Mum, feeding the toaster. 'But will Mr Dandow?'

'Grandpa Catt will tell him,' said Eva, because Grandpa Catt was dealing with things.

'He'll tell Mr Dandow,' said Mum, 'but I don't care about him; I care about Gideon,' and she gave him a friendly thump.

'Booey,' said Gideon, meaning Mummy, and 'Baooh', that he was happy.

'Well, I suppose we ought to have regard for Mr Dandow,' said Mum. 'It is like he was captain of a ship, a bit more than Grandpa. A bit more than Daddy, if he was here just now.'

The toast was ready. Gideon took back the butter and used it. Tansy and Mercury came downstairs in their pyjamas and prowled round the table. Mum looked at them, hoping they were not there just yet. 'I keep thinking they are imaginary,' she said. 'Specially when I can't remember their names, which I got out of a book and it went back to the library, so no wonder I don't remember.'

Gideon took a bit of toast, then dropped down on the floor to give the little ones a ride round the table, three-legged because of the toast in the hand of his front leg. When he had been round once he stood up, and they fell off, shouting at him indignantly.

There was a grunt and a squeal outside, and on the kitchen wall appeared strange distorted writing of an unreadable character, surrounded by a red glow and accompanied by a royal coat of arms in reverse. Something skittered across the floor in the passage. The writing on the wall floated away and the red glow vanished. The postman had delivered and the low sun had reflected from the side of his van its captioned heraldry wrong way about.

Eva went to find what had been delivered. She was discovering that it was a postcard addressed to her, not Mum, when Grandpa Catt came in the back door.

'Morning, my love,' he said. 'Postcard from your Dad, is it?'

'Val ... um,' said Eva, not getting the name of th place at one go.

'Valparaiso,' said Grandpa Catt. 'As like as no' who's here, then? Morning, Daphne, my ´ Gideon, ship's boy. What do you think to t'

'He hasn't thought of it at all,' said Mum.

Gideon said nothing. He felt happy towards Grandpa Catt and needed to say nothing. The little ones climbed on Grandpa Catt. Mum read the postcard.

'Changed ships,' she said. 'About five weeks from now should get back. It would be a help if he put the date, for I can't decipher the postmark.'

Gideon finishing his toast and kicking every step on the way upstairs to dress.

'He'll sink the boat,' said Mum.

'Dandow knows,' said Grandpa Catt.

'Gideon doesn't,' said Mum.

'I'll have a cup of tea then we'll go down,' said Grandpa Catt.

Mum poured tea, remembered the names of Tansy and Mercury, and sent them to dress.

That, thought Eva, is why I know what Gideon was like when he was small: like Mercury. 'Was I like Tansy?' she asked.

'Like one of them,' said Mum. 'More like the one with straight hair, not the one with curly hair.'

'Mercury,' said Eva.

Upstairs Gideon washing and singing, and a great slop of water on the bathroom lino. Gideon coming down soaked to the elbow, his curly hair damp and pointed, his glasses splashed.

'Come on,' said Mum. 'Gideon come and get a job and do work. No, not clearing the table. No, we go down to the canal. You're sure he won't drown in the canal, Grandpa?'

'It isn't his depth,' said Grandpa, making a level not far above the table with his hands.

'I saw something swim across it this morning,' said Eva. 'To the other side.'

'He could walk across on top,' said Grandpa. 'There isn't much depth to it anywhere.'

They set off into the brightness of a sunshine higher than it was when it smashed Eva, and multiplied a thousand and a thousand times in the rain suspended from the leaves of all bushes and trees. Looking back as they went down the road, Eva saw Mercury scattering universes on Tansy as he plucked at overhanging sprays, and Tansy wearing in her hair galaxy after galaxy.

Beyond them both, beside them all, the canal and the more distant river were cut out of the sky, the same bright element as those stars.

'Hoonph,' said Gideon. Gideon marvelling at these things, or meaning he had an expectation of ice-cream. He expected something fresh out of his day and Now.

CHAPTER TWO

Gideon taking Mum's arm with his fingers, striding out, head up.

Mum loosened his gripping fingers and slowed him down. 'We'll get there all the same if we walk steady,' she said. Gideon had a happy smile. He was happy. Mum got her arm away from his fingers and tucked her hand under his arm. Together they ran along the road a little way, down the slope, and then walked again.

Grandpa Catt followed. He had Tansy and Mercury on one hand, because they would not settle for one each until he gripped them into submission. They were dressed at last in the fragments of cloth they used as magic cloaks, draping them over their shoulders, where they gave power.

At the bottom of the hill, Gideon began looking about for the shops among the houses at the edge of the canal. Mercury and Tansy joined him. Mum turned off the power supply to their cloaks, knowing where the switch was.

Grandpa Catt took over now. With him in charge there was no thought of ice-cream for anyone. He had arranged things for Gideon, and had to get Gideon to want to do them. Gideon and Grandpa Catt got on well together, and so did Grandpa Catt and Gideon, which is not quite the same thing. Eva would have liked Grandpa Catt more to herself, but Gideon simply took up more time than most people, just being Gideon.

They all went across the road and into an alley between houses. At the end of the alley there was a dock running off the canal. Here a great dullard boat wallowed in greasy water, steam at the stern, smoke at the roof, the engine running. Then the boat brightened within and became decorated, electric light shining inside, coloured and sharp. Red and gold lettering at the forward end and across the stern said SHIRE CASTLE.

Mr Dandow was on board, his black hair cut close up the side of his head, the flat sectors of his face shaved high before his ears, all his hair on top, and himself looking forward with flat eyes. He had switched the lamps on.

'Right then,' he said, 'what dost think? Come aboard and have a sight and see what he do think, eh? Mrs Catterell, Walt.' Walt was Grandpa Catt.

'That's it, Bob,' said Grandpa. 'And I'll get out and do the work, like for to show, and he'll catch on and help and then be doing it himself.'

'Because we can't explain ahead of time,' said Mum.

Tansy and Mercury were on the boat already, like a set of pirates. 'Cast off,' said Mum. 'We'll go home.'

'Hey there,' said Mr Dandow. 'Keep them out of the bar.'

The boat was a canal barge made into a cruiser for sightseeing trips. It was ten feet six inches wide, it said on a beam, and fifty feet long. It had a superstructure with glass windows all round, and two rows of seats like a bus. At the front there was a snug saloon with a counter and shelves of bottles. Here were the coloured lights glittering among the clear drinks.

Mr Dandow stayed high at the back, to steer, and to control the engine.

Mum took the shoes off the pirates. They walked on the cushions, leaving steamy outlines. They shouted for fuzzy drinks.

Grandpa Catt was last on, casting off ropes and stepping aboard as the boat moved off.

Gideon looking over the side for wheels.

'He knows it's a bus,' said Mum. 'And he's right, of course.'

Eva knew it was a boat, and thought she could prove it from seeing a bottle of rum in the bar.

'That's it,' said Grandpa. He knew. He had been a sailor before Dad. And now Gideon was to be one, perhaps, but much nearer home than Valparaiso.

Mr Dandow called from above, and slowed the engine. The boat turned out of the dock into the canal, with Grandpa out on one side with a pole in case they drifted into the canal wall.

'Nothing hard about the turn, not really,' said Mr Dandow, 'but oftentimes you get a plastic bag or rope or rubbish on the shaft or the propellor, and she do lose way and might go straight on sideways and sink, and there, I'd have to give the money back.'

'He didn't take much notice of that,' said Mum. 'Did you, Gideon?'

Gideon looking for the stairs, wanting to go up on the top deck.

'Single-decker,' said Mum. 'On this route.'

'Low bridges,' said Mr Dandow.

Then Gideon being a little anxious because there was no driver at the front. He did not expect the lack to cause a crash, but knew what was right. Grandpa stood him in the entry port and showed him Mr Dandow at the back, holding the tiller.

'Is this going to work, then?' said Mr Dandow.

'Oh yes,' said Mum. 'Gideon ahoy! He doesn't forget, but of course he doesn't know yet, but he's working on it. He's deaf, so we can't tell him a lot, and he has brain damage, so he's slow, and there's some things he won't ever know, we believe. But he's clean and particular and happy, and it'll be all right if you give him time. Just now he's thinking it's like a bus, and it's hard to tell whether he thinks it should have wheels, or whether he just wants to point out that it hasn't, in case we haven't noticed.'

'I'd never given it a thought,' said Mr Dandow. 'Now, there's the first bridge, Walt, if you want to have a go.'

'I'll have a go,' said Grandpa. The engine slowed again and the boat came close to the canal bank. Grandpa

17

jumped off into the grass and jogged along the towpath. 'Hold her back,' he said. 'This is all I can do on land.'

Mr Dandow held the boat back, a hand on the tiller, a hand on the throttle, his eyes looking at Grandpa, navigating from the highest place on the boat.

Grandpa drew ahead, reaching the bridge first. The bridge was low, half a metre above the water, so that no vessel could have run under it. Grandpa drew up two latches at one end, and swung the bridge round from the other by turning a wheel. The boat slid by, Mr Dandow's head turning to watch the bridge.

Gideon watched too. So did Mercury and Tansy. What they were saying was not clear, since they said different things at the same time. Eva thought they must be in a spaceship, cloaks on line again, bound for Novendore in the book she was reading.

'I can see he's twigging it,' said Mr Dandow. 'And,' looking at the little ones, 'I hope he comes by himself.'

'He's twigged it,' said Mum. 'Will he do it, that's all.'

Grandpa came jogging up after the boat and climbed on board, the bridge closed again. Gideon was delighted when a car came down the road and crossed the bridge.

A swan came pedalling by. Gideon very interested in that and its system of legs. Eva felt that he was sure the boat had something of the sort to move it along.

There was nothing for the swan, no sandwiches, no cake.

At the next low bridge Gideon watched Grandpa's feet as he stepped off the boat, and as he stepped on again. 'More,' he said. 'More.' Then he had to hit the side of his head because of the noise in it.

'I'll go first, next time,' said Grandpa, 'and next time I won't go at all.'

That worked well. Gideon followed Grandpa, was very fussy about the latches of the bridge, very firm with the wheel, got back to the boat first, and helped Grandpa on board. 'Thank you,' said Grandpa. 'You go first next time, Gideon. You don't need help from me.'

'Baooh,' said Gideon, and at the next bridge pushed Grandpa to one side and went on his own.

'I thought he could, Bob,' said Grandpa.

'I'll take him on a trial,' said Mr Dandow. 'He'll get his money like anyone. It's regular turns, wet or fine, mind, and good time-keeping too, can't wait around.'

'More,' said Gideon.

'More coming,' said Mum, pointing ahead to where something crossed the water again.

'A lock,' said Mr Dandow. 'More to do there, and sometimes going upstream and sometimes down, into the river beyond. So good so far, but you got to think through a lock.'

The boat came under the long curved wall of Shire Castle, which it was named after, and into another abandoned piece of ground, derelict like Edenfields. Road and rail bridges crossed above, and empty quays and landing stages faced empty water.

Beyond the neglected yards and tracks on the left bank lay the river.

Grandpa worked the lock when they came to it, Gideon hands-on with him. Eva, not knowing any more about locks than Gideon, but knowing other things, was alarmed when the boat went through the gate and began to sink. But the water sank with it, when the lower gates opened. The water changed from the dead clearness of the canal to the live cloudiness of river.

Grandpa and Gideon came aboard again, and the SHIRE CASTLE went down the living water, under the traffic bridges, under the grey girders of a span where huge pipes looped the water, through a cavern under the railway, where starlings flew.

At a wide basin among other boats Mr Dandow swung the boat about, and they worked back the way they had come, towards the lock. Gideon leaping out and working the lock and the bridges as they came, waving the boat through, captain of each one by one, captain of the boat between them.

At the last bridge he helped the little ones out as well, and they rode the turning roadway, Gideon showing his authority, but being sure they had no part in his rightful work.

'Can he use a bike?' asked Mr Dandow. 'He's to run a long stretch between locks when we go further downriver into the city docks.'

At the SHIRE CASTLE's own dock Gideon tied the boat up, when he had seen Grandpa start the work. Gideon tied a bow but like a shoelace, the only knot he knew.

'Well, 'twill hold,' said Mr Dandow. He carefully shook hands with Grandpa Catt only, ignoring Tansy and Mercury, who wanted to do the same. Wearing magic cloaks they thought they could grasp his hand and hurl him over their shoulders into the canal, a thing they could not manage to do to each other because both expected it. Mr Dandow had been told to ignore Mum as well, in case Gideon became jealously protective and be unable to leave her.

'You stay,' said Grandpa Catt to Gideon, giving him to Mr Dandow.

'Come home for tea,' said Mum. 'I mean at tea-time – no, off you go now.'

'I'll manage he,' said Mr Dandow, leading Gideon off. He had the first trip of the day lining up on the dockside, waiting with Mrs Dandow to go aboard and sail away.

'He can walk out of the job any time,' said Grandpa. 'Afloat or ashore. But most likely 'tes now or never.'

'We'll stay a moment,' said Mum. 'In case.'

Eva thought, He must: he is my own brother and he must do all he can; he has to succeed. But it is all Now to him.

The boat moving, Gideon in the hatchway, standing at watch, peering ahead for the bridges to come, knowing they were there because he had seen them. Eva saw him looking away from her and Mum, and realized with a sudden warming of the eyes that they were abandoning him, and he was forgetting them, and that it was right. As he swung his head from side to side, hearing noises in it again, she saw sunlight condensing in the lenses of his glasses, brightness before his eyes.

'Valparaiso,' she said, or the word said itself. We both understand, she thought, and sniffed.

They had ice-cream at the shop on the corner, and went home, up the hill, the sun high and commonplace, the water dried from the leaves.

The little ones, sensing the difference between solid world and fluid boat, stood with closed eyes until they fell over, then held their breath until they burst ten seconds later. They had ridden the boat over universal seas.

Gideon still riding it.

CHAPTER THREE

At the gate of the house next door stood Mrs Lear, furry slippers, white apron tight into a crease between her lower and upper bulges. She smelt of fresh pastry. Her cottage was level with the one where Eva lived, but the road had gone down the hill by then, so there were steps up through a little garden.

'Has he gone to the school again, Mrs Catterell? Gideon, I mean.' She said Catt – er – ell and Gid – e – on, all the syllables tumbling from her mouth quick but separate, glinting in Eva's ear, because Mrs Lear had always been Welsh.

'The school was good,' said Mum. 'But this is better than the school. He's working.'

'Working,' said Mrs Lear. 'Working proper?' And the

words sang out and rubbed themselves into tinkling dust up the hillside of Edenfields.

'Working,' said Mum, telling herself as much as telling Mrs Lear, warm and proud, and her word not lifting into the air at all. 'Happy as a sandbag,' she added. Eva thought that was some sort of mistake, but said nothing about it.

'Working,' said Mrs Lear again. 'What is he doing then? It isn't everything he can do, with the best will in the world. Come in and tell Mr Lear.'

Tansy and Mercury were through the gate before it was open, and past Mrs Lear, though she was wider than it, climbing the steps like water pouring upwards, babbling as they went.

'I'll come as far as I can see the road from,' said Mum. 'Gideon might set out home again. We think he's settled, but it's hard to tell. Wake up, Evie, standing in the road.'

Eva woke up. She found she was suddenly taller than Mrs Lear, and could see along her parting, dark hair, light, light skin of the scalp.

'I'll just go home,' said Grandpa Catt. 'Work to be doing.'

He was building the next house in the row, actually the fourth, because Eva's family lived in the second and the third, most of which Grandpa had built too.

In Mrs Lear's cottage, fire burnt in the shining black and brass of the range, the golden kettle chirruped at the hob, Mr Lear chuckled in his chair on the hearthrug, a geranium seemed to grow black against the bright window. A square china plate on the wall asked God to *Bless the House*, and another said, *Praise Yea the Lord*.

24

Tansy looked in a cupboard, Mercury looked in a jar. 'Goodness,' said Mrs Lear, 'nothing for you today.'

A standing clock took a deep breath and spoke ten times loudly. Tansy clung to Mercury, Mercury to Tansy. Their cloaks were no defence for them – they were not used to being shouted at. When the clock had spoken severely to them they went to stand in front of it, gazing at the stern pendulum that indicated their guilt, as it leaned to Tansy and then to Mercury. The kitchen fire showing as an angry eye on its polished bob.

'They're hypnotized,' said Eva.

'Are they?' said Mum. 'I should have had them done before.'

Mr Lear was speaking, not much more noise than the wheezing of the clock, without tick or tock or strike. 'Work,' he said. 'It's good to get and bad to do, work. Not coal-mining, is it? That's where I began, down to Radstock.'

'Not him,' said Mum. 'He's on the canal, opening the bridges and that.'

'Then he'll be bringing the coals,' said Mr Lear.

'Tourists,' said Mum. 'That's his load. He went down for the first time this morning, which is why I'm looking down the road, in case he comes back too soon.'

'Horse boy, is he?' asked Mr Lear. 'Poor soul.'

'A hundred years behind the times, is Mr Lear,' explained Mrs Lear.

'He thought it was a bus with legs,' said Eva. She meant no unkindness, mockery, or laughter, but Mrs Lear took her up at once.

'He's as God made him, and I'll poor soul him as well

25

as Lear does, but I won't jeer. If God made him he's God's work. You have to think of that. It's in the heart and not the head, see, and if it wasn't, well, he thinks as real as anyone, even if he can't say it so clear. There's many a thing been said in this world that no one understood, greatly full of meaning.'

'Some souls are different,' said Mr Lear, breathing out a few words more. 'You can only speak for your own.'

'But what I say doesn't always go accordingly with Lear,' said Mrs Lear. 'Big nonsense man, he is.'

'We'll go,' said Mum. 'I can see those two revivalists are about to hatch, and I'd better get them caged. You get one, Eva, and I'll take the other.'

The two revivalists grew so heavy (it was one of the strange powers of their cloaks) that no one could lift them. Once again Mum switched cloaks off.

'There's a bit like that in the book I'm reading,' said Eva. 'On the planet Novendore, but it was actual gravity and there wasn't a switch.'

Later on, while Grandpa Catt sliced and laid gritty mortar high on the new walls, Tansy and Mercury took all the loose rugs out of the house to make a tambourine or trampoline. No one was sure which, since they jumped on it as well as beating tunes out of it with their hands.

'He'd have loved a baked-bean sandwich,' said Mum, opening a tin at dinner time. 'But he would have eaten it before he got to the canal.'

'He won't starve,' said Grandpa Catt, washing his hands in cold water, for preference, at the sink.

'We'll see tomorrow,' said Mum. 'We don't know

whether the habit has set in yet. He might walk in now –
he may not know about time, but he does know about
dinner.'

Eva made white toast for the little ones, gold for herself
and Mum, and hardbaked for Grandpa.

Afterwards Eva tidied up the dishes. Mum sat down
and did nothing. The little ones had taken their plates
out to a den as soon as they got them. Somebody would
find them later, black slugs on the pink plastic, stray
beans rotting.

'It's lovely,' said Mum. 'I'm sitting here without him
and no one is bothering me. But it's not like when he was
at the school, or on the Club holidays, so I'm bound to
worry. There he is, working away on his own, and he
must be liking it or he would have been back by now,
and he might be set to work for ever, and that's good.
Because he does pin a body down so, and mothers do
grow out of their babies, really, long before the baby is
bigger than the mother. But just think, if I could get it
right, what a peaceful day to have a rest.'

It was. The clear afternoon hung over the quiet valley
hidden at the back of the town. Inside, the comfortable
shade was rich with light. Now and then a car went by
on the road. Distantly, though only next door, Mr and
Mrs Lear sang a hymn. Over Edenfields the hum of insects
held the day together.

Grandpa put brick on brick, the slush of mortar
dropping on each time, the brick tapped level, the paper-
tearing noise as the spare mortar was trowelled away,
and a sort of spit as it went back on the heap.

Mum had ten minutes of doing nothing, then went to

27

help Grandpa Catt. Eva went to help Tansy and Mercury, because it was obvious that one needed help to rescue the other from the one, but it was difficult since they kept changing sides with each and their own selves, and there was not much room for strangers who did not know the language.

Mum was mixing mortar when the noise started. Grandpa Catt was saying, 'Don't lift your shovel off the ground – slide 'un and turn 'un,' and Mum spoilt her stroke by knowing what the sound was and reacting to it, then knowing that the sound could not be what she thought it was.

'Just like Gideon in the wars,' she said. 'But it must be someone else.'

'It do sound very like, though,' said Grandpa.

It was. It was Gideon coming through the house with his hair flattened, Gideon lifting his feet as he walked because his shoes were uncomfortable, Gideon shouting for Mum to put things right, Gideon spluttering and wiping his nose with his sleeve.

Gideon dripping water everywhere, soaked and still soaking. Mr Dandow followed behind, not looking very anxious.

'Walked off the boat, he did,' he said. 'Soss into the water, that old canal. So I thought to bring him back. He didn't give it a thought until he got in the house.'

Gideon's teeth rattling. Gideon enjoying that new feeling, but still making a great bleating. Mum took him away upstairs, pulling his clothes off as he went, water running into the bath.

'It shouldn't hurt him, that,' said Mr Dandow. 'They

all step in sooner or later, walking in at the sharp end, like.'

'We all done it,' said Grandpa, looking at the mortar trowel and ready to go back to his work.

'My missis done it,' said Mr Dandow. And he and Grandpa Catt thought about Mrs Dandow in the water. It was a satisfactory thought. Grandpa looked at Eva, and she knew she must not laugh, or even think about Mrs Dandow and water.

'He'll be down in the morning,' said Grandpa. 'Certainty.'

'Or I'll come,' said Eva. 'I would.'

Upstairs Gideon getting into the bath and beginning to crow and sing. Mum came down carrying wet clothes. Water lurching about overhead.

'Can you manage? Evie could . . . But he'll be all right. He was ready to start back, but I've taken his clothes.'

'Morning, then,' said Mr Dandow. Then he went, turning his van briskly in the road, straight-sided head turning sharply like a robot's behind the screen.

'Evening,' said Mum.

Gideon sailing his bath through a rough sea, water leaping, Mum going up to quieten the waves.

Then the little ones had found the mortar, something they had planned all their lives, it seemed. Gideon lost his long warm soak, and gritty little ones were dropped into the water instead.

'Eva, come and hold them under,' said Mum. Eva took her book about the planet Novendore and sat on the bathroom stool, while the characters she was with inevitably went into the great magnetic cave from which there was no return before the bad-tempered sun, Qualor, burst with terrifying fury.

Gideon fell asleep at tea-time and put himself to bed. In the morning Mum was awake first, for a change, and made him get up and go as far as the bathroom, but he would not dress or get out of bed again.

'He's all right,' said Mum. 'Obeying his instincts, that's all.'

Gideon shouting 'Hyagh' for hunger. Gideon eating his breakfast, then lying in his bed with his glasses on, looking at the ceiling and going to sleep quite often.

'Worked hard yesterday,' said Mum. 'Stiff as a board, I dare say. Just going down to the kitchen, Gideon,' she told him.

Gideon saying 'Booey', which meant, 'Mummy's duty is to stay here in this room and look after me, but I shan't make a fuss about it if you wish to neglect me.'

'I know exactly what he means,' said Mum. 'Evie will stay with you. All right?'

'Voy,' said Gideon, which meant, 'Eva will do as a poor substitute, but I had expected better things.' Then he said, 'Barbosch,' and Eva obediently brought Paddington Bear to sit beside him.

Without giving Eva the chance, Grandpa went to the dock and did Gideon's work for the day, coming home dry outside but, Mum said, wet inside.

'We had a drop when all the tourists had gone,' said Grandpa.

'They'd better not give Gideon anything like that,' said Mum.

Eva thought it could not be worse than the orange

squash the little ones had had all day and which did not last long. About twenty minutes, Mum thought. 'More or less straight through. It would be more economical if it could be collected and used again, because it can't have changed much in the time.'

'I think it maddens them,' said Eva, because during the afternoon, when she sat with Gideon, reading about the planet Novendore, they had ravaged her own room, living in her bed (a raft, a tent, a cloud, a tambourine?), tipping out her collection of sea shells and treading one to death, scattering her glass beads, leaving orange squash stopped on her dressing-table.

When she complained they chattered at her in mysterious tongues, and ran amok in Gotham City.

'We're outnumbered,' she told Mum. 'Hasn't it ever occurred to you?'

CHAPTER FOUR

Grandpa thought it would be fair, seeing that he had had such a day, for Eva to help him move some bricks down from the piece of wilderness called Edenfields, at the back of the houses.

'That leaping ashore for the bridges is too much at my age,' he said, 'come to think of it.'

'It wouldn't be fair,' said Eva, who thought that her day was over by now, with being on duty with Gideon, having her room invaded by aliens, and not being able to do what she would have liked best of all those things, the bridges on the canal. However, beyond saying several times that it wouldn't be fair, and getting angry about it, there wasn't any way of explaining.

Grandpa Catt became moody too, and went off alone

to do the work, leaving his last cup of tea quivering on the table.

'But it isn't fair,' said Eva to Mum. Mum filled the kettle noisily instead of speaking. Eva felt guilty about the whole world, about Gideon, about the little ones, and in particular about Grandpa Catt. And being quite certain about the unfairness made the guilt worse, not better.

'They left your room a pigsty,' said Mum. 'Do you want to tidy it, drawing Gid's curtains on the way and putting back anyone who has fallen out of a top bunk . . . ?'

Eva was unable to do any of those things immediately, because there was some confused argument inside her still. She walked up and down the kitchen for a while. Outside, in Edenfields, Grandpa tipped a barrow-load of bricks.

'Why don't you send them to school on the planet Novendore?' Eva asked, when things had become more neutral.

'Is it a different school?' asked Mum. 'It would have to be different, never mind the planet.'

'I don't know what it's like,' Eva said, and then paused, because her voice was still enraged and hard, and tried again. 'I don't know what it's like. It's just a long way off and they wouldn't get there until the third generation. And if you sent them now it would only be a half fare.'

'If they go by train,' said Mum, 'it's free.'

'I'll go on reading my book,' said Eva. 'The sun Qualor is about to burst in horrifying splendour, but I expect it's because they've been tinkering with it.' And she went upstairs muttering Tinker, Tinker, and found them sprawled on their beds, as lovely as they were awful, and tucked them in.

Gideon was asleep like a log. In her own room it was obvious the sun called Squalor had burst with stupefying untidiness. She cleared things up, fetching flannels from the bathroom to clean away sticky patches. Protoplasm, she thought, remembering what lived in Novendorian caves.

As she sorted beads into their kinds, shells into their breeds, she heard Grandpa outside, gathering bricks where the brickworks had been, and bringing them to the house next door, first into a rough heap, then into orderly stacks. She could not watch him, because of feeling guilty again. He just wanted me to help, she thought. And he isn't actually awful, or of course lovely, but he's just the same as the little ones. Then she thought she was fair about them, at least, who could put their sweet arms about her neck and their interfering fingers in every corner of her room.

Gideon woke up a little and shouted 'Booey' for Mum to come up and say good-night.

Eva drew her own curtains. Grandpa Catt went on working outside in the darkness of her mind, the long summer twilight.

In the morning Gideon climbed out of bed and dressed. He rubbed the backs of his legs constantly, but he was ready to go to work.

'We'll all go down with him,' said Mum. 'Then some-times you can take him on the way to school, and some-times I can, and that'll be easier until he goes on his own.'

Tansy wasn't being dressed that morning and went down in her nightie and magic cloak, with the sun shining straight through her. At the dock Gideon pushed Mum and Eva away, and went to work independently.

Gideon beginning one of his long jokes, with Mr Dandow, about falling into the water, demonstrating with his hands how it had come about; time after time.

'It'll go on all day,' said Mum.

'He can tell the tourists as often as he do like,' said Mr Dandow. 'But I don't think he'll fall in again, not Gidden.'

They left him waving his hands and rubbing the backs of his legs.

'I really think he's all right,' said Mum.

At home Eva went quietly out into Edenfields and filled the barrow with bricks from the tumbled heaps among the little trees. Grandpa climbed down from the house wall and wheeled the load down for her. No one said anything about duty and fairness. Mr and Mrs Lear sang soothing hymns all morning, and in the afternoon stoked up a great baking-fire. Mr Lear had to walk, as threadily as his voice, out into his garden and sit there with his stick, watching Edenfields, but perhaps seeing no detail now at all.

Gideon came home by himself. He had three ice-cream cornets in one hand and three in the other, and was licking them as he came.

'Where's he got those?' asked Mum, sharp.

'Wages,' said Eva. 'You get wages. You don't have slaves any more. Don't spoil his fun. Or perhaps they're for us.'

'He hasn't been paid yet,' said Mum. 'And they aren't for us, with him licking them down like that. Where did you get the money, you great greedy thing?'

'Hoonph,' said Gideon, slyly, like a dog that knows it has broken the rules.

He finished the last crumb of cornet and grinned, licking his lips. He belched.

'What do you expect?' said Mum.

Gideon now held his stomach. His grin went quite away, and he grew pale, waxy like a candle. He groaned and held his throat.

'I wonder how many he's had, six or sixty,' said Mum. 'Get out of the way; I think we're going to rush to the bathroom.'

'Booey,' said Gideon, painfully.

'Get up there,' said Mum. 'If you're sick on the floor there'll be a row, I can tell you.' Someone knocked on the door. 'Get it, Evie. If they want me they'll have to wait. Move, Gideon.'

Gideon moving, lumbering up the stairs, bathroom door closing on him and Mum. Eva not listening any more.

Mr Dandow was at the door. 'Mum in, my love?' he asked.

'She's with Gideon,' said Eva. 'Upstairs.'

'Oh dear me,' said Mr Dandow, and Eva saw his flat-screen eyes lift a little as he listened upstairs. 'That's what it come to, then. There he was, telling this yarn all day, and they were all giving him money, cash, see, and he had a few ices when we come back in the dock, and at the end he spent all he had, I reckon, eating them wholesale, and I come up as soon as ever to tell your Mum, but I see she found out. Tell her I be sorry, but if he got a mind to do something, well, he's very like to do it.'

Gideon went to bed soon. 'More like sixty,' said Mum when she came down. 'But still, no harm done, no actual damage. But I wouldn't have sold him so much, and that's what I'll tell her at the kiosk.'

Gideon got himself up for one errand. He came downstairs pale, and still dribbling. He had collected together the remains of his money, all coins, and now put it in the sink among some potato peelings.

'Rauh,' he said, meaning it was something he no longer cared for. He took himself back to bed. Later on Mum took the coins up to his room and put them on his table. Next morning they had gone.

'He got over that,' said Mum. But it was not so, in fact.

CHAPTER FIVE

The little ones prattled in their sleep at first light, cocooned in their covers and only their jaws moving, each seeming to understand the other in their chrysalis code. Eva was aware of them as she woke, was used to them: they would talk a long time before waking into their dreadful flying selves, hurraying with their heels, bumping against wall and ceiling, shaking the house.

Gideon shouting before his eyes opened, his waking. Gideon getting out of bed, dressing; up for another day of freedom from the world. The night is the only time he is the same as the rest of us, Eva thought. Even the little ones are best asleep. But if we did not know them awake we could not think of them asleep.

Gideon going downstairs, shaking his head, hitting it

38

with his arm. Gideon saying 'Dthth' to the kitchen, and then calling 'Booey' for Mum.

The little ones emerged from their beds completely winged and deadly. They stayed in their room. They began a revolution with heavy armament and large numbers of troops, each soldier with one leg, hop, crash, bang and screams. Beds were being crushed, windows broken out, floors torn up. There must be smoke.

Mum took no notice and went downstairs. Eva opened the door with caution, expecting the inferno beyond, a whole country laid waste, hedges uprooted, a dark daylight coming through the roof of the house.

Tansy and Mercury were both on the top bunk having a quiet tea-party. The room was tidy. They were drinking from pieces of paper.

'Hot water,' said Tansy.

'Dancing tea,' said Mercury, waving paper.

They took sips of this tea and began to sway, laughing. The bunks began to sway with them, hitting the wall, lifting from the floor. The drinkers shrieked. They made the bunks throw them off. Eva caught them and tried to dress them, but they ran downstairs with nothing on, racing round the kitchen where Gideon was waiting for Mum to provide breakfast.

'Rauh,' he said. 'Rauh, rauh,' expressing his disgust at their appearance. But he said 'Dthth' to Eva, glad to see her.

Mum took the Dancing Tea addicts away. Eva made real tea and toast soldiers for Gideon, with hard edges so that he could crunch with his teeth and hear something. Stereophonic food was what he liked best at meals.

39

'Is he going to work?' Mum asked, when she came down with the little ones.

'As far as I can tell,' said Eva. 'He's stowing in enough for a week.'

'I'll make him a sandwich to take,' said Mum.

Gideon going upstairs and cleaning his teeth loudly, spitting with the whole head. Leaving the tap to run, not able to hear it, unlikely to see it.

Eva went up to fetch him, to take him to the dock. School began again on Monday, so she could always take him on week days.

She took Tansy and Mercury as well, in the magic cloaks. Mum had made them sandwiches for breakfast, and they had a picnic by the rubbish bin on the dockside (dropping their crusts absently in), drinking more Dancing Tea from the wrappings before throwing those away too, then murmuring 'Hoonph, hoonph,' having caught the word from Gideon and hoping it was magic for them too. They shouted it at last.

Gideon noticing and saying 'Rauh' at them from the end of the boat, where he was sweeping the roof. It was all he said to them this morning.

Eva, the cruel overseer of the death march, led them home, ignoring tears and broken hearts and stomachs empty because they had not eaten crusts. There was no ice-cream.

At home they locked her behind a wall two bricks high and left her to perish. She was allowed to go for breakfast after promising to perish later. Tansy and Mercury went to show Mr Lear great marvels.

Grandpa dug half-buried bricks from the undergrowth,

cracking off old mortar and dropping them in the barrow. Tansy and Mercury came to help, but were diverted by having to hunt a woodlouse across many yards of forest, as if they had not seen such a thing before. Perhaps the woodlouse had forgotten. In the end it appeared in two places at once, and then brought itself together before things were too complicated.

Then Tansy had a small green caterpillar in her hair, and went to show Mum the new friend.

Grandpa tried to hose down the muddy bricks he had gathered, keeping invaders at bay with a flick of the wrist and a flurry of spray. His array of thin bricks reddened and brightened under the water jets. The little ones, threatened and frightened, ended muddy but not very wet. They turned the hose on each other and then through the back door.

When Mum came out they went to live among the trees of Edenfields.

Eva went further into the caves of Novendore. Towards the end of the afternoon she went down to the dock for Gideon.

'I don't suppose he will spend anything on ice-cream, and that's all he would buy,' said Mum. 'But it's pay-day and let's see he gets the money back home, because I want to get him to pay some rent and keep, now he's earning.'

Eva went down the road pondering on the unfairness of earning money, and then not being able to keep it because people charged you for living in your own house.

She was down at the dock early, and waited for the

boat to come back. She watched it swing in from the canal, preceded by its own swell of ripples, and draw alongside.

Gideon saying 'Dthth', and slapping the back of his head where it buzzed and sang. Gideon leaping off the bow, taking a rope with him, looping it round a post.

The boat stopping and the stern swinging out. Gideon on board again, trapping another post with a rope at the stern. Gideon helping the passengers out, saying words that Eva had not heard before, meaning, 'I hope you have had a pleasant trip and will come again.'

'And,' said Eva later, when they were wondering about money, 'he was copping a few coins and stashing them in his pocket. They like him, of course.'

However, at the quayside, Gideon seeing his customers off, then going round the boat shutting up the windows along the side, tidying the glasses away into the bar, tipping ash into the canal from the trays.

Mr Dandow stopped him, because his work was done.

Gideon standing in front of Mr Dandow, who took Gideon's hand, opened it, and carefully put into it quite a lot of paper money and a little heap of silver and bronze coins, closing Gideon's hand on it all.

'Take it home,' he said. 'Home.'

'Voy,' said Gideon, meaning that he would agree if he knew what Mr Dandow was saying.

'Home with it,' said Mr Dandow. 'Right?' And they both waved hands and arms about to show that they agreed about something, though it might not have been about the same thing.

Gideon smiling towards Eva, nudging his glasses into

42

place to see her better. Gideon stepping on the boat again for some last-minute work. Eva went to get him. Gideon coming ashore again without having to be asked.

Gideon saying 'Hyagh', meaning he wanted his tea, rubbing his ear and saying his loud tooth-vibrating 'Nnnnnzzn' to chase sounds from his head.

On the far side of the canal some boys fishing shouted and screamed and laughed and ran away all at once, clutching some catch they thought valuable or unusual.

Gideon at home, having had no thoughts of Hoonph, turning out his pockets for Mum. He had several silver coins and a lot of bronze. But he had no bundle of paper money at all.

'But I saw him get it,' said Eva, cross with him for mislaying it when it had not been out of sight, when she had watched him all the time. 'Mr Dandow folded it into his hands like a present. Then he came home with me, and I'm sure he didn't drop it.'

She remembered the sequence of things, how Gideon had stepped back into the boat and then ashore again. How his hands were empty then, and she had thought he had put the money into his pocket.

The boys the other side of the canal with their net, taking a catch that delighted and surprised them.

'He threw the paper money in the canal,' said Eva. 'The same as he emptied the ashtrays in there. He thought Mr Dandow gave him some rubbish to get rid of. That's what he did.'

'It should still be floating,' said Mum. 'It would, wouldn't it?'

'It won't go far,' said Grandpa, readying to stand up. 'No current in a canal; the water doesn't go anywhere.'

'No, it's gone,' said Eva. 'A lot of little boys the other side caught it in their net and ran off with it. I know, I saw them do it and heard them run away, and I sort of wondered then, because they've never caught anything before.'

'That's it,' said Mum. 'He'll have to start paying his way next week instead of this, and Mr Dandow must pay him in coins only, and we'll get those back without any trouble unless he Hoonphs. Meantime I'll send Tansy and Mercury out to mug all the little boys, because they do that naturally.'

Gideon going out of the house and into Edenfields, and coming back for his tea.

'We'll have what you've got, anyway,' said Mum, when she found him again and emptied his pockets. But they were already empty, though she had previously seen nearly a pound in silver and bronze in there. First the paper money had gone, and now the metal.

Gideon ending the week with nothing, not even his tea so far, sitting at the table and saying 'Hyagh' impatiently.

'It's that ice-cream,' said Mum. 'He's turned against money because of that, and we'll never see it. It's not just a habit now, you know how he is; it's a fact of life.'

CHAPTER SIX

A letter for Mum fell through the letter-box. The van went up the hill while the rooms of the house blushed. The letter was thick in a floppy airmail envelope with a chocolate stamp, possibly not real, a long letter from Dad describing where he had been (South America), and saying he would send a message when he got nearer home.

Mum settled down to read it five times through to begin with, and then carefully.

'I keep thinking it will expand and tell me more each time,' she said. 'I'm sure they could do it if they tried, electronic paper. It could keep sending the message as it changes. Now it's like a clock stopped, always says the same thing even if it isn't true.'

45

Gideon down and saying 'Booey', but getting little attention from Mum. 'Hyagh,' he said plaintively. 'Nnnnzzm.'

'Evie will make toast, Gideon,' said Mum. 'I'm reading my letter. No, Gideon, this isn't your letter, so put it down, leave it alone. I shall shout.'

Gideon sitting down and leaving the letter alone with his hands, but his mind still working on it. 'Rauh,' he said, and tapped his head, pointing to Mum. 'Dobithor.'

'I don't know what that means,' said Mum. 'Is it a bargee word?'

'Tansy and Mercury say it,' said Eva, stacking the toaster and pulling the handle down.

'I should know,' said Mum. 'If he can get the meanings without hearing the words, then I should be able to translate back into language.'

'In Novendore they speak Intergalactic,' said Eva. 'If you won't send them, why don't we emigrate?'

'If I knew what it meant I'd know whether I wanted to know,' said Mum.

'They read it somewhere,' said Eva. 'Didn't they, Gideon?'

'They can't read, write, or even talk,' said Mum. 'And where are they, and please will they stay there?'

When the toast had sprung out and steamed on Eva's hand, she went to find them. Mercury had packed Tansy into a pillowcase and was delivering her to the elephant. You either understood at once, or never at all, what the scenery of their life was. Mercury was convinced he was already dressed in the sumptuous clothes of the elephant, and Tansy reckoned the magic sack was a practical morning garment.

46

Mercury came down sobbing with the pain of wearing trousers, and Tansy was totally affronted by her socks, but achieving dignity by dragging a grimy pillowcase behind her, with herself in it, you were to understand.

'Thank you, Evie,' said Mum. 'I'll deal with them now.' But it was clear that Mum would read the letter first and last and between times, and was among those that had to be looked after, not among the usefully occupied.

Eva dished out cereal, toast, wipes with dishcloth, sugar, reproofs about eating like dogs. 'Elephants,' said Mercury, blowing milky bubbles out of his giggling nose.

Mum on the high seas, syllabling each wave of the voyage, saying each sounding, a long way from port.

Gideon sitting in his chair drinking his tea, knowing it was Eva's duty to supply him with food when Mum was busy.

It was a satisfactory occupation for Eva, being responsible for them all for a time. But she had to dress and go to school. She came upon the limits of being one person, having many thoughts but capable of only one activity.

'Don't be late,' said Mum vaguely, when Eva was ready to go. 'Can't you take them all with you?'

'I would if it was the school jumble sale,' said Eva. 'You're supposed to buy your own stuff back. Come on, Gideon, let's get you down there. Are you coming?'

Gideon shaking his head and thumping it, and following her, not wanting to walk so fast as she had to. She got him to a lumbering run by the time they were at the dock.

Gideon shaking his head, not liking to run because it

made him dizzy. He pushed her away roughly and growled. She hit him with her school-bag.

It was a short quarrel. She had to stop, open the bag, and give him his sandwiches.

Mum always took several days to recover from one of Dad's letters. 'It's the climbing out of the envelope,' she said. 'Has anything been going on while I was in there?'

'Didn't miss you,' said Eva. 'Get back in and lick the flap. I'll write the address on, Novendore. There they have machines that read for you and understand too, no bother with language. Like Tansy and Mercury.'

Mum stayed out of the envelope, unaddressed and unstamped, cooking and cleaning, able to notice and cure Tansy and Mercury of the habit of getting on the table to have their meals, like some picnic. She did not mind where they were, but thought they should not warm their feet on the teapot, because the weather was not cold.

Gideon coming home day by day and having a little sleep before his tea.

'I hope he isn't overtiring,' said Mum, looking at him. 'He's losing a bit of weight, and that won't hurt. Is he eating his sandwiches, do you think?'

Gideon opening his eyes and blinking at her, saying 'Dthth' and then listening to some sound no one else could hear, something beyond language, beyond meaning; useless.

'Hyagh,' he said, ordering his tea from Mum.

There was a light drizzle outside today. Eva went out to stand in it, watching Grandpa Catt increase the wetness with the hosepipe, sluicing a batch of newly dug bricks.

The little ones came out. Grandpa went to turn off the hosepipe. Before he did so the sun came below a cloud and put light on the last droplets of his spraying, so that they shone gold against the wet glimmering green of Edenfields. Then there was more than gold, as it broke into the bands of the rainbow, standing in the air close against them all, part in the air, part in the eye. Grandpa swung the spray to trace the whole arch, and then the house itself bit the sun off, and there fell only rain without colour.

On Gideon's pay-day the rain still fell. Mum had meant to go down to the dock and make sure of things. Mr Dandow had promised to pay in gold pounds and other coins. In the rain, not knowing the exact hour that Gideon would finish, with the two little ones to tote, Mum did not get to the dock. She saw Gideon only when he came in and sat down.

She made him get up at once and take a wet coat off. Then he sat again and stretched a wet shoe to the fire and watched it steam.

There was no money.

'Dandow will have it,' said Mum. 'Is that it? Where is it, you great thing? Did he give it to you? What've you done with it?'

Gideon sleeping with his shoes cracking at the fire, Mum hauling his legs to the side. The little ones came and sat on him while he was inert. He would nowadays only play with them occasionally.

'The way a lady rides,' said Tansy, cantering breathless.

'A way a farmer rides,' said Mercury. 'Bumpetty.'

'Dumb,' said Gideon, waking and pitching them off and falling asleep again. They went to dismantle the stairs.

'He remembers all sorts,' said Mum. 'He just can't get it together. I wonder about that money.'

In the morning she went down herself to Mr Dandow and spoke with him before the day's journeys began.

'I filled him up with no end of big coins,' said Mr Dandow. 'No paper, like you said. But what's my responsibility, I'd like to know? If he has wit enough to work then he has wit enough to carry the money home, I reckon. And best call those kiddies away from the edge there, Daphne, or we'll have more splash than enough.'

'He's had wit enough to hide it away,' said Mum. 'That seems to be it. Well, don't you trouble; we'll just have to keep watch the day you pay him. It'll be something too simple for us, in the end.'

'He didn't pitch it in the canal,' said Mr Dandow. 'He don't say much, but is he making up for it in thought? I can't tell.'

'He will be,' said Mum. 'I'm sure.'

'He should,' said Mr Dandow. 'He've got our job taped, bridges and locks and all, as good as any fellow yet, and like I say, no backchat and that. Deserves the money, he does, earns his rivets, and gets them given.'

'And then it's his,' said Mum.

And that's actually fair, thought Eva. His's is his.

CHAPTER SEVEN

'He doesn't seem to come to any harm,' said Mum on another wet day, when Eva came home dripping and they were waiting for Gideon. Eva hung herself on a chair and looked imitation pathetic, being not the same as Gideon, who did it better than a dog.

'Nor do you hurt,' said Mum. 'We're a waterproof lot.'

Gideon coming in at the front of the house, having been run up the road by Mr Dandow. Mum scampering quickly up the stairs for a towel for him and drying his head; Gideon grunting at her and grabbing for his glasses, which she had removed before rubbing his head, and was now drying in turn; Gideon speaking to the fire in the front room: 'Dthth,' and shaking from his ear water and then sounds; Gideon settling into a chair, thumping

51

his head quiet, saying 'Nnnnzzm' loudly and falling asleep.

Mum flapped the magic cloth at the little ones and drove them upstairs. Water gushed, children yelled with rage and delight, and Mum came downstairs, still waving the magic towel. She put it in Eva's hands.

'Just keep an eye on them,' she said. 'I'll bring you a cup of tea,' and she filled the kettle.

Outside the rain fell steadily, raising a mist from the ground, settling in for the night.

It is the ending of the day, Eva thought. It's one actually crossed off existence, a failure. She switched on the bathroom light and it shone on the wet shoulders of the little ones. Nothing more, she knew, could happen that day; and after tea she would read, because there were no days like this on Novendore.

Downstairs the kettle whistled. There seemed to be a crocodile in the bath, from the reports coming out, biting off legs and consuming soap.

Mum brought tea for Eva and orange juice for the little ones. It was not allowed in the bath, for hygienic reasons. She pulled out the plug on them, and they were being sucked down the plug-hole, backside first, making giant noises.

Downstairs Gideon slept through the uproar.

'Zonked out,' Eva said to herself, though out loud. She was thinking, This is a man, and my brother, and he is more real asleep and less real awake.

The front door rattled, as if a wind had sprung up in the road. It opened, and a man came in.

'Dennis?' said Mum, startled. 'Dennis.' It was Dad, dark

52

in the dark hall, with so little light from outside and nothing from the house.

Upstairs the bath was in agony. Down in the hall Mum ran to Dad and held him until water ran down her neck from his beard, and she had to stand back and rub him and herself dry, and give Eva a chance to come near.

'Taller and taller,' said Dad. 'Even a short time do make a difference.'

'Some tea first,' said Mum. 'I'll get it, Evie. I just want to run a comb through my hair, a sight. I look a sight, I know; you'll think I don't care how I look.'

'Nothing to fret about,' said Dad. ' 'Tes my girl all the same. You won't have my telegram, or whatever sort of thing it is now. That'll come after I've arrived, tomorrow, from Lowestoft.'

'Just a big letter a week since,' said Mum.

Gideon waking up and staring at the fire, not hearing noises near him; sitting up and looking round when Dad came into the room; saying 'Hyagh', beginning to say he was hungry and changing the word to a greeting, pleased to see Dad, shaking his arms and making him sit down against the fire.

'Well, Gid,' said Dad. 'Good, eh?'

Gideon telling stories. It was a dumb show with noises, of going into a house with wheels in the water, with chairs in it and bottles with lights, and how machinery was worked to turn the bridges to one side.

'Keeping up nicely,' said Dad. 'Has he just been today? Fair old day to start out.'

'Every day,' said Eva. 'Not Sundays. Grandpa Catt fixed it.'

Gideon telling about machinery Eva did not know.

'Laundry, turning mangle?' asked Dad.

'Lock gates,' said Eva.

Gideon falling into the canal with great drama, getting up soaked in carpet; Gideon telling the story of falling in and getting money; Gideon eating too much ice-cream.

Mum said, 'You can stop there. We'll guess the next bit, thank you.'

'Wait,' said Eva. 'He might tell us what he does with the money.'

But now Mum was back the story stopped. Mum went to sit by Dad.

Gideon not thinking that was a good idea, Mum's place being exclusively by him.

'Booey,' he said. 'Baooh.'

'Mummy sit by Daddy,' said Mum. 'Daddy's turn.'

'Watch and watch about,' said Dad. 'Seamanlike.'

'Rauh,' said Gideon.

Upstairs someone was now stuck in the plug-hole, a little flank being sucked away, and calling for help in a piteous giggle.

'Who'll go?' said Mum. 'Batman or Robin?'

'Popeye,' said Dad, running quickly up the stairs.

There were two screams, two people bounding down the stairs, pink and clinging to Mum.

'There now, what is it?' she asked.

'Whiskers,' they said, rolling their eyes.

The whiskers came down the stairs and sat down beside Mum again, and small persons dived to the far side.

Gideon, offended by seeing Mum sit next to Dad, disgusted at the little ones with nothing on, went to sit in the kitchen with Grandpa Catt, who was waiting to finish his mug of tea and get away home, but giving the family a chance to see their father before he saw his son.

The little ones remembered how whiskers would tickle tummies, and were on the table walking them into it, while Mum tried to stow stray legs in night-clothes.

Gideon saying 'Hyagh' very often in the kitchen, and an occasional 'Rauh'.

Grandpa Catt came through. 'Going all right, then?' he asked.

'Middling and better,' said Dad. 'Just an extra week now, but longer later on.'

'Shouting for his tea out there,' said Grandpa Catt.

'I know,' said Mum. 'I'll have to move and get it. Grandpa Catt, you'd better stay too, welcome anyway, but Gideon just a bit jealous and it might help.'

'I'll step down to the Navigator's Arms and bring back a jug of ale,' said Grandpa.

No one knew what the little ones thought ale was, but they fell to the ground and rolled about laughing with tears on the faces, repeating the word.

Gideon still with his insistent 'Hyagh' in the kitchen.

Grandpa went out wet and came back wetter. The jug of ale had a plastic bag over it. To keep it dry, perhaps.

Mum tried to feed the little ones there and then and put them away for the night, but they were incapable of seeing outstretched bread or spoons of egg, and turned their heads right round like owls to avoid the sight, their mouths closed except for the necessity of breathing or releasing essential giggles. Tears of concentration and effort fell from their chins.

'Was I like that?' Eva asked, failing too to feed any morsels.

'You were dead normal,' said Mum. 'Exactly the same. No one should be any different. Gideon isn't different either. He has the same problems as anybody else, the same feelings. He can be unhappy, but perhaps he can't be so happy as anyone else, not get quite so much out of it, not having so many things in it.'

'Sometimes,' said Eva, speaking from experience, 'unhappy is perfect.'

'Maybe,' said Mum. 'What shall I do with two cold soft-boiled eggs? I know, sandwiches for Gid in the morning; no, not now, Gid.'

Gideon was still in the kitchen. Eva and Mum could see that he was pretending to himself there was no Dad in the next room playing with the little ones. Gideon was in here, being with Mum. His place. 'Voy,' he whispered.

'He gets so jealous,' said Mum. She tried to send him upstairs to have a bath, but he would not go. 'Nice lovely sosh-sosh,' she said. Gideon merely growled.

He stayed in the kitchen when the food went beside the fire in the other room. He ate both cold eggs and the fingers of bread and butter. Mum went through to talk to him; Grandpa went through to coax him; the little ones went to draw him in with a babble of fancies he might like; Dad thought a touch of the man-to-man might persuade him. They all failed.

Eva went through last and gave him a stack of plates to carry in, while she brought the pie.

Gideon thinking of the work he was doing, carrying as carefully as Tansy or Mercury (if they ever did such a thing), forgetting what was in his mind otherwise, proudly putting the plates in front of Mum and sitting down in his usual place, looking as if his back had turned numb when Dad put a capturing hand on his shoulder.

'Hoonph,' said the little ones, looking at pie and custard.

'No hoonph,' said Mum. 'I think it's still a bad memory for him.'

Afterwards Eva walked through a starry Edenfields with Grandpa Catt, with the rain stopped from the sky but playing among the trees where the leaves had retarded its fall, and all the ground bubbling underfoot. She wanted to explain that Gideon's behaviour was not Gideon's fault, and that if she did not speak for him no one would know what he meant or felt.

'As for that,' said Grandpa, 'he should tire of his Dad. I tired of mine, and yours tired of me; but go away and come back and that do make the world go round. But Gideon gets it a hard way, for he can't leave home, and has to have it with him for ever, or for a long time. You're the only one fit to leave, and not ready for that yet.'

'I often feel like it,' said Eva, looking up among the stars for Novendore, without seeing its name. But Grandpa Catt did not know of places beyond Valparaiso.

Indoors, Dad was asleep. Mum had put the rest to bed, and was now determinedly washing dishes.

'No,' she said, when Eva began to help. 'Go to bed. If I was doing this because I'm Mum I'd be furious, but I'm

57

doing it because I'm the only one awake, so I don't mind. But all the same, I expect I'll bend a plate or break a spoon.'

Eva kissed her and went to bed. Tansy or Mercury in the next room went on eating with open empty mouth.

Old dog Gideon snoring gently in his bed.

Rain fell again outside. Downstairs Mum talked to Dad. The house was full.

CHAPTER EIGHT

Gideon struggling to stay awake when he came home from the canal. Gideon not wanting to come out of sleep and find Dad there again. Dad gone a week now, but Gideon still wary after his days of affront.

'Glad to see him at first,' said Mum. 'Then he gets possessive. I've looked after him so much he thinks he's the only one.'

'He doesn't mind us,' said Eva. 'Or more like he doesn't take any notice.'

'There's a long time ahead,' said Mum. 'There'll come the day when I'm not here at all.'

'Dead,' said Eva. Mum was at that moment cleaning the gas cooker, lifting grease from the ferny coils of pierced pipe under the hotplates.

59

'If you put it like that,' she said sharply, banging a frond of metal into place, 'if that's how you want to say it.'

Eva opened her mouth, found it was saying nothing, and went away to visit the little ones and Grandpa Catt. She supposed she had kicked Mum somewhere tender and had been kicked in turn, though not anywhere in particular.

From outside she heard Mum rebuild the cooker with a series of hard blows, then light each ring with little claps of thunder.

Grandpa Catt was putting his ladders up on to the first level of scaffold to stop Tarzan and Jane climbing the high trees of his poles and swinging down with bat-like squeals. At the moment Mercury was chimpanzee to Tansy's Tarzan, and Tansy ape to his. The two of them could quite easily be all four at once.

'And who are you?' said Grandpa. 'You don't look like anyone at all.'

'She's in a mood,' said Eva.

'She is, after your Dad goes back,' said Grandpa. 'She'll turn right before long.'

'I know, in actual reality,' said Eva. 'I understand. She's got to do it to someone, and she doesn't do it to Gideon, so that's all right.'

She seemed to have done it to the little ones, who sat down to their tea with great attention, and even ate pieces of salad put before them, without a word. Eva thought they could tell they must by the firm way the tomatoes had been sliced.

Gideon leaving his, saying 'Rauh', and then obeying a look Mum gave even him.

The little ones, thinking they must have done something wrong, climbed on Mum and on Gideon and on Eva, each one being in three places at once, until everyone felt suddenly desperately happy with what they had, and desperately sad at the same time about losing Dad to the sea for the next month and a half.

'Washing dishes next,' said Mum, recklessly, filling a bowl with water at the sink and dropping Mercury into it, starting a fearful riot.

'As bad as them,' said Eva, mopping the wet floor and sending Mum away to bath the little ones in a more usual way.

Gideon banging his head and saying 'Dthth', 'Rauh', and 'Baooh', being pleased, disgusted, and eager for more.

Grandpa Catt came in to see who was left alive.

The next day was Gideon's pay-day. Once more no one managed to be there when Gideon had his heap of golden, silvery and bronze coins given to him, and he came into the house without anything.

'He got here before I set off for him,' said Mum. 'We must get it right next week. And we'll find out where he's put the last few lots, one of these days. I want some housekeeping and he wants some savings. He might as well save when he can, because he'll never make a big wage.'

Eva went to see whether Grandpa knew anything.

'Nothing,' he said. 'And believe me, I've looked, there isn't a brick in Edenfields left unturned, and for the most part used up. Tomorrow I'll start dismantling that old hearth, and I don't know that's plenty to finish the job.'

'If you ask me,' said Eva, 'the house will be a ruin before it's finished. Of course,' she added, since it was possible to turn Grandpa sour for a time by saying the wrong thing, 'some ruins are famous.'

But Grandpa was thinking away on another tack. 'All the bricks in this row of houses came out of that hearth,' he said. 'And many a house more. So it's still working, all these years gone. And I never saw Gideon's money. You'll have to watch him, that's all.'

A week later Eva held her mind on the thing she had to do, watch Gideon, and was ready, out of school, going down to the dock at the earliest possible moment.

The dock was deserted. There was no queue for another trip; there were no customers at the ice-cream kiosk; no traffic came down the road; the public house across it was closed; the boat was not there and not in sight.

There was a little drifting wind, carrying with it blocks of damp, not rain, not mist, but a sort of wettingness. No one needed a coat. The dampness seemed to moisten the smooth lozenge-shaped ripples of the canal, making them need a rub with a cloth to get their shine back.

Mrs Dandow was in the office belonging to the canal cruises. She was busy with a typewriter. Its clatter came across the quay like the scurrying of some creature in an underground pen, ringing a bell at each corner.

SHIRE CASTLE came slyly up to the quay, the engine bobbling away at the back of it quieter than the type-writer, dropping into a non-working state of noise, and stopping entirely. And a sort of silent echo shimmered from neighbouring buildings.

Gideon opening the door in the side with his big hand,

62

standing in the hatchway as the boat came to the stone landing. Gideon stepping off and walking to the back of the boat, reaching out to take a rope from where it hung against the boat's black stern, looping a bight of it round a bollard.

The boat checked against that. Inside it, behind the damp-starred windows, the trippers began to stand up and come to the door, the heads of little people showing dark and light as they talked and moved.

Gideon signalling them to wait, a pushing-back gesture, Gideon very much in charge, the people pleased to obey him, a teacher and her children.

Gideon going to the front of the boat. Gideon seeing Eva as he went, where she sat on the edge of a raised flower-bed, not wanting to move because her legs were warmly together and her hands drily clasped in her lap. There would be a moment at which to leap up and rescue money, but it was not yet.

Gideon reaching for the bow rope, grinning at Eva. Gideon dropping the rope and reaching for it down below the edge of the quay.

The boat coming against the stones; little lapping of water between it and the land; a small scraping, or grinding, sound.

That will cut the rope, Eva thought.

An unearthly noise began somewhere, a machine mad with disrepair, some part of it shrieking against another part. Eva's hands grew cold one against the other.

Gideon rolling on the wet stones. Gideon with his mouth open, Gideon struggling against some unseen enemy, howling at some extreme hurt, holding a hand against himself, holding it away from himself. From him the shrieking; his the wild sound.

Mr Dandow running along the side of the boat, taking up the rope, jumping ashore, tying the rope down, kneeling by Gideon.

Mrs Dandow ran out of the office, her summery dress clinging to her when the damp wind licked with its dew. She put the little gangplank in the doorway of the boat and began to help the people out. The school of small children lined up clutching hands and walked away to a waiting bus and departed, leaving a stink of diesel smoke.

Eva was up at once when she saw Gideon hurt, and running to him. Mr Dandow held him by one arm and had wrapped the other in a cloth from the boat, a bar towel saying 'Lager'. Gideon lying on his back, still yelling, rain dimming his glasses on the outside, tears flooding the inside.

''Tes hurt, 'tes hurt,' said Mr Dandow. 'His hand, my dear, 'tes his hand. Run up for your mother, there's a good maid, best to have her. This be a hospital job, crushed hand, betwixt boat and quay, all the full weight of the boat. So you run up and get she, my love, then.'

Eva hesitated, unable to leave Gideon, unable to stay, dithering. Gideon's breath coming in great sobbing sighs; Gideon not knowing where he was hurt, blind with tears, blinded with rain.

'Run on, then,' said Mr Dandow sharply. 'You be no manner of use here.'

Mrs Dandow was bringing a rug from the boat, and a little bottle. Both Dandows knelt in the rain by Gideon. Eva pushed her bag of books under her arm, ran across

64

the dock, into the road, and up a trickling gutter towards home.

Water ran down her neck. Inside her neck her throat stuck, and she knew she could never say words when she arrived; she would stand dumb, no manner of use there either, forgetting she had learnt to speak.

But it was not like that. She opened the house door and tumbled in. Mum met her at once, pulling on her coat.

'Where is he?' Mum asked.

Eva's stiffness of throat ran down her body and changed to a tremble of the knees. 'Hurt his arm,' she said, holding the door open.

'Little ones, Mrs Lear,' said Mum, going out through the kitchen to the back door. 'Grandpa Catt, where are you? Not here today. Tansy, Mercury, come on, walkies. Evie, get coats on them.'

'Barbosch,' Eva said.

'I'll get him,' said Mum, two steps at a time up the stairs to get Paddington. There were shrieks after her to get Mooli and Delfont for the little ones. Mooli was a primitive action man from before there were wars, and Delfont a piece of blue blanket with six knots, two buttons, and a row of extra blanket stitch along the belly, thought by Tansy to be the centre of the world's mysteries.

When they were ready it was quicker to take the little ones down the road with them, since both of them and Mrs Lear would have had to be introduced to the notion that they were to stay there for a little time; and it might not have worked in any case.

Gideon at the dock lying just inside the office, Mrs

Dandow holding his good hand, the other still in the bar cloth. There was now red on the cloth.

'Dandow have gone for the van,' said Mrs Dandow. 'Supposing you do want to be up to the hospital, seemingly, so he will take you.'

'Oh yes, oh yes,' Mum was saying, crouching down beside Gideon.

'Laying there so white as a maggot,' said Mrs Dandow.

Mum looked inside the cloth and covered the hand again. She swallowed and her jaw went tight across the cheek.

Gideon seeing her, knowing she was there, wanting to lift that hand to hold hers, unable to do so, and not thinking of using the other one.

Tansy and Mercury looking with interest at the cloth, then walking Mooli and Delfont up and down Gideon's legs. There was no space in which to take notice of them: everything now centred on Gideon.

Mr Dandow brought his van round and opened the back. 'Can we get un up?' he asked. 'Will he walk?'

Gideon being lifted to his feet, and the feet and legs not working. Gideon reaching for Paddington and saying 'Barbosch' with his lips but not his voice; shaking his head, wanting to bang it with his hand, unable to; but, with that occupying his attention, his feet walking.

'There's a bit of old soldier, you ask me,' said Mr Dandow. 'He don't be hopeless hurted.'

'Not today,' said Mum. 'But enough. There, Giddy, you sit in the back here.'

While he was being manoeuvred Eva was sent to the boat for seat cushions, making a layer in the back of the

66

van. Gideon going in, Mum after him, then Eva to support the other side; and last of all the little ones in dribbling yellow coats, wet Mooli and sodden Delfont.

Mr Dandow closed them in and drove off, with loud music coming out of the speakers.

Gideon, like a dog, whimpering, all eyes without his glasses.

'Can't wait,' Mercury decided, at a traffic light.

'Yes you can,' said Mum, slapping his knee. 'And that's for starters. I know about you.'

Tansy took a deep breath and decided to say nothing.

The hospital breathed disinfectant at them, and a sort of bar smell. Gideon going away on a stretcher, with Mum and Paddington, leaving Eva with the little ones and Mr Dandow.

'I can't wait,' said Mr Dandow.

'Yes you can,' said Tansy, hitting him on the knee.

'Hey,' said Mr Dandow. 'But I'll come up when your Mum do telephone, and here's the number, see,' and he went away.

Eva managed to thank him before hauling the little ones to the hospital toilet, down an endless arched corridor where nurses trotted on their own reflections and there was a smell of school dinner, not hospital.

Mum came back an hour later without Gideon, but with a nurse, who brought her a cup of tea. The nurse said they understood the problem with Gideon, and they would manage, because he would not be doing anything that night but lying asleep.

'You drink the tea,' said Eva. 'I'll ring up Mr Dandow, and he said he would come up again for us.'

Mum looked for money, and came up with coins to put in the telephone and the biscuit machine. 'You'll all be starving,' she said.

'Orange juice,' said the little ones. Their ears sort of lift up, thought Eva.

'No drink,' said Mum. 'Too many traffic lights on the way home.'

At that moment Grandpa Catt came walking in, with his good trousers on, and a clean jacket, and a tie.

'I've brought your transport,' he said. 'Where is he?'

'In the ward,' said Mum. 'Asleep. He crushed his hand.'

'I've seen that happen,' said Grandpa. 'Nasty. Then what?'

'You have to hear,' said Mum. 'They had to take off two fingers.' She looked at her own hand. 'One of them,' she went on, putting her hand out of sight, because to see it and speak of what had happened was too painful, 'one of them right back to the wrist. And,' she went on, with her voice shaking, 'he bled like a little pig.'

Then she was crying into her tea, and the little ones were kissing her with biscuity mouths, so that she laughed and snuffled. Eva stood next to Grandpa, looking away down the wide corridor, not sobbing, but with tears running down either side of her nose, and down inside it as well.

A man nurse came to ask whether he could help them, but Mum said she was as happy as she could be, and glad 'twas no worse, as if that made any matter.

They went home in Mr Dandow's van, Grandpa Catt having borrowed it and driven it up. Mum sat in the back with the little ones, Eva in front with the gear-stick shaking in its socket and rapping her on the knee now and then.

'I can wait,' said Mercury, resignedly.

'You'd better,' said Mum, and then everyone in the back had hysterics. In the front Eva and Grandpa Catt exchanged looks and drove on in a serious manner.

But the house was not full tonight.

CHAPTER NINE

No morning shout from Gideon in the house in Edenfields; Gideon not getting from his bed and walking downstairs.

Eva heard the different silent, which had woken her just as well as the noise would have done.

There had been silences before: every year Gideon went on his holiday with the Club; but this absence was not the same. Eva woke more than usual, wondering whether she should go down to the kitchen and start the world. She lay still and considered whether all the strings of the day were in tune. The bass string of the day was not here: Dad was on his ship. The next string up, Mum, was used to playing his note as well as her own, and she was here. Eva tried her for pitch, and thought she would do. The third string, Gideon, was not there: broken, Eva thought; not there but echoing all the same. There was herself, a string she did not hear. And the strange descants of the little ones above the bridge, elfin, remote, but piercing.

Tunes could be played; sounds would come out.

Sounds began to come out. Tansy and Mercury began to buzz, to throb, to vibrate, to beat the drum. All at once they stopped. Their door opened, and Eva heard their stumping tiptoe across the landing, and sort of twittering (certainly the wrong side of the bridge) at Gideon's door. They had looked, and not found him. Of course they knew he was not there, or they would not have looked. If you don't understand that, thought Eva, then you don't understand anything. They came to Eva's bed and climbed in with her.

They both had to be taken to the bathroom at once, not being capable, they said, of finding their way there from Eva's room. After that everyone was up and in the kitchen.

At the stairtop Gideon's room lying vacant, the bed abandoned and stiff, the window unused, the clothes in their cupboard ownerless; the whole hollow room adding an echo to the house.

Gideon, later in the day, lying in the hospital bed like an empty thing, echoing the hospital, his arm in a huge white mitten.

Gideon happy; Gideon king here: the nurses liking Gideon: Gideon having new words for them: saying 'Gaboo'.

'He knows a gaboo when he sees it,' said Mum.

Gideon saying it to anyone who came marching by,

71

and introducing Paddington, who lay beside him with bandaged paw of his own: 'Barbosch'.

The little ones went about saying it to other patients: Eva saw them cowering beneath their sheets after several of them had been zapped.

A nurse came to feed Gideon, because his right hand was the hurt one.

'Don't let him get soft,' said Mum. 'He's the biggest eater with both hands, so he can manage with either. Go on, leave him, or you'll never get away. Come on, Gid, you great lump, serve yourself.'

'Voy,' said Gideon.

Tansy (or Mercury) tied Mercury (or Tansy) to the end of a bed. Eva was not acknowledging either of them today because they were both being kinky. Mercury had his hair full of ribbons and his jeans on back to front, and Tansy wore the fighting hat from a soldier suit, insisted on having her zip undone, and said her name was Boy.

We could make an appointment to have them corrected, Eva decided. But maybe I have an eccentric family. And she looked at Gideon.

Gideon sitting up beaming; Gideon sure he was the centre, the full centre and not the slightest bit off, of all the attention and purpose of the ward; Gideon having already acquired more cards and messages than anyone else. Nothing from me, thought Eva. Nothing from us. But all the visitors and all the nurses seem to have left him something.

The number increased while the family was there. A woman came in looking for him, the boy who got hurt on the boat. She brought a home-made card with about forty names on it, and a picture of a boat, with Gideon driving. The woman was the teacher of the children on board the day before, and the card was theirs.

'We talked about it this morning,' said the teacher. 'I thought we shouldn't run away from it, and we've done drama, and mass-and-momentum and writing and art. And here's a card.'

Gideon waving a spoon at her, saying 'Gaboo'.

'Probably goodbye,' said Mum. 'But that isn't all he means by it, I'm sure. We don't know anything he means by it.'

'Signs of a rich inner life,' said the teacher.

'He likes a bit of fuss,' said Mum, not quite wanting to talk about him to a stranger.

The little ones were having a rich inner life too, but had to be unfastened from their bonds and rushed along the corridor. Today both of them might have been indignant, taken through the door marked Ladies, if they had been able to read.

Gideon being happy when they left him, with everything being done for him.

'He'd lie there for ever,' said Mum. 'Actually he would miss his Mum more if they hadn't given him something to stop him being awkward.'

At home the little ones went into a bath, and Eva did not have to care what they did. She left them to Mum.

Grandpa Catt was outside, wheeling up a load of sand that had been delivered. 'Settled in, has he?' he asked.

'Better than home,' said Eva. 'He's got all the nurses tame so he can eat from their hands. Apart from that he isn't doing anything.'

'What about *his* hand?' asked Grandpa, sandcastling a barrow-load. 'Is that all right?'

'Nobody said,' said Eva. 'Must be fine.'

'Good, then,' said Grandpa. 'Time to knock off for me, I think. I'll just come in a moment. And Saturday tomorrow. I thought we might break into that hearth and pull out some bricks to get on with.'

Mum said they had to be careful up there, because the hearth was old.

'All the outside is baked into a lump,' said Grandpa. 'But I'll take care.' Then he left, and Mum began to think of food.

'It's been on my mind ever since I saw Gid getting it stuffed into him,' she said. 'If I'd got hold of the spoon he would have had to share, I was so hungry.'

Grandpa came back in again. 'I forgot,' he said. 'Dandow came up with a great pocket of money for Gideon.'

'What I went down for yesterday,' said Eva.

'It's the first we've seen,' said Mum. 'My goodness, it's a fistful, isn't it?'

Grandpa was tumbling coins out on the table, dull bronze, bright silver, thick shining gold.

'It's a good feel, the solid stuff,' said Mum. 'We can do with this.' And she gathered it up, stacking it on a shelf, because the bulk was too great for her purse.

The next day was relaxed, at the beginning. Eva woke thinking of Gideon, and at once knew where he was and how he lay, and how he was and where he lay. His room was not so empty of him now she had seen him in another. She could transpose him as she wanted, complete with all his cards and gaboos and Paddington.

Mum felt the same. 'I like the holiday,' she said. 'I do.' She was still more happy when a letter came from Dad, and she settled to read it her great number of times.

Eva breakfasted the little ones, who had got up normal, and then insisted on lying on cushions on the floor to eat breakfast, wanting Eva to spoon toast into their mouths.

After this recumbent meal she took them out to talk to Mr and Mrs Lear at their garden gate, Mr Lear pink and white and still, on a garden seat, Mrs Lear red and black and clucking Welsh at them, like one of her own fowls.

Grandpa Catt came down from his house to the brick-hearth, and began tapping at the bricked-up arched opening with a pointing-pick, the noise bouncing across Edenfields in the still morning.

Eva left the little ones and went to help.

'If I just get driven in,' Grandpa said, 'then I can pull out one by one. But it won't [thud] drive so easy if it's [ding] solid in there [crumbling crush]. Ah, there it goes, a bit of room inside, or that wouldn't have [rattle] fallen in.' He was hurling back fragments of brick, putting in the point of a bigger pick, and levering.

Bricks fell round his feet. He stumbled on them as he stepped away smartly, in case the whole hearth was coming down round him. But only the filling of the arch had stirred.

'Well, that's a barrow-load,' he said. 'Fine and ready to use. I hadn't properly seen, but these aren't built in, no mortar to clean up, no trimming. These have been stacked dry, so they'll lift away and build at once, when

I've wheeled them down and lifted them up where I want them, which is the big part of building.'

He took a load down to the house. Eva stacked more for him, pulling them away from the loose wall. Beyond this outer leaf was another wall, not built right to the top of the arch, and probably easier to start on.

The little ones disposed of Mr and Mrs Lear by telling them everything they knew, which they were good at listening to, and came up in the barrow with Grandpa Catt, after the eighth load.

By now the outer layer of bricks had been shifted. Grandpa pulled at the next stack, lifting bricks down in pairs, filling the barrow, then continuing with the demolition to see what lay beyond it.

Inside the hearth bricks stood in a honeycomb, spaces lying between.

'Well, they'm fresh,' said Grandpa. 'New as milk, and a shame really to have all fresh brick near the housetop after all that weathered stuff lower down. I d'wish I'd been in here before.'

He decided that everything was safe enough to let Tansy and Mercury come to see. They clambered up fallen brick and looked in. Eva waited her turn. She felt her quick look from outside was going to be enough: a brick is a brick. But the little ones always expected the next look to be decisive, the turning-point of their lives, and they went in eagerly.

They looked in and babbled about some inner life that came to them. Then their noise stopped in mid-babble, in mid-sound, mid-breath, unnaturally. They stood as if they had been turned to baked clay themselves, silent, still.

76

They began a whispering scream, a sizzling in the throat, like pensive hens, and their heads started to swing from side to side, slowly, as they watched something on the floor below the bricks.

'Come down,' said Eva, because she thought a great silliness was starting. But neither of them could move.

'What is it?' she asked Grandpa Catt, becoming uneasy, because this was not silliness, and what could there be in an old hearth?

They went up to look. Going up to look meant filling the archway with heads and shoulders, making it darker inside and harder to see what was there, what moved across the floor like a layer of water.

The hearth was full of snake-like creatures, writhing and turning, gliding over one another, moving back from the light, earth-coloured, smooth, narrow-headed.

'Blindworms,' said Grandpa. 'The place is like a tomb with them. You should see 'em in the vaults to the churchyard some time. Edenfields is the ground for these little snakes, too. I heard they bite cows, but not people.'

The little ones did not hear. They were transfixed. There was nothing else in their minds at that moment but the joy and horror of what they saw; they had nothing to say but the chattering scream, the sound coming up from their throats, into their mouths, and among their even, childish teeth.

They had to be lifted down and taken indoors to Mum, gasping, 'Worms, worms.' Mum remembered what the teacher had said the day before, and played snakes with them, did drama (pastry cakes) and made drawings.

'Two is worse than forty,' she said. 'And they don't

leave at half past three; they just go home, which is, stay here.'

By half past three they had recovered, and went out with a plastic container to catch a snake for snake pie. When it stings us, they said, we shall sting it. They told Mrs Lear as well, about snakes and their stings.

They brought back only a button, which they took to Mum, who thought it would not be useful because it had no holes in it. 'Probably why it fell off,' she said, stacking it with Gideon's money on the shelf.

Grandpa went to find them a tame blindworm. They had changed their intentions now. What they wanted most of all was the stack of Gideon's money. They climbed up and brought the metal tower down on themselves, ending with their little faces bruised in thin and thick lines by the falling edges. Eva did not know whether she laughed with them, or cried, her face wet.

'I expect that's all,' said Mum, when the little ones and the coins had been gathered up. 'But I didn't count them.'

'There's two,' said Eva.

'I can do that on my fingers,' said Mum. 'I mean the coins.'

The two dropped tears over Grandpa's found worm when he brought it in, the feelers of its tongue licking their fingers. Mum gathered up yet more coins from the floor, like dead leaves. Two human worms coursed the hearthrug.

Eva took the blindworm outside at last. She set it in the grass and it went to cover against the fence, then through the wire to the other side, where Mrs Lear's hens pecked it up and swallowed it in unthinkable finger-lengths, each one twitching down a bird's throat.

Eva went in unable to eat, not daring to feel anything. But her day was not over, and the worm's day was.

CHAPTER TEN

Gideon in the front seat of Mr Dandow's van, Grandpa Catt driving from the hospital, waved off by Gaboos. At each halt in the journey Gideon telling someone outside why his hand was bandaged; how many Gaboos had attended him; that he could manage bridges.

Gideon coming home.

Gideon sleeping on a long time in the morning, no shout from him, no thumping first down the stairs. Gideon coming in to breakfast when everyone else had finished.

As you might say, thought Eva. But Mum did not have breakfast, Eva had finished her own before getting to the table and sitting down, and the littles ones were in a patch of sunshine outside with cereal bowls on the ground, lapping like dogs.

Gideon saying 'Dthth' and waiting to be served, expecting to be fed, unable to use his left hand now he was home.

'Suit yourself,' said Mum.

Gideon laying his bandaged hand on the table.

'Look at the poor pathetic stump,' said Eva.

'He's spoilt rotten,' said Mum. 'But let him get on with it now. He's clever enough to be as stupid as he likes. Come on boy, it's a hard life, I know, but get it eaten.'

Eva went to school. Coming back in the afternoon she met Gideon in the road, Gideon agitated about something, and with a much smaller, untidy bandage on, as if he had thrown some of it away and the rest was soon to be lost.

It was not the bandage that bothered him, but something to do with the boat. Gideon standing in the road not knowing which way to go.

'Come home,' said Eva.

Gideon banging his head with his hand, hearing the noises, saying, or roaring, 'Nnnnzzm, nnnnzzm,' but going home with her.

Mum and Eva pieced it together, with a long show from Gideon explaining what he had seen.

'He had a sedative in hospital,' said Mum. 'They'd have to, to keep him happy. That's why he slept in this morning. But it's worn off now, and then what, Gideon?'

Gideon acting out what he had done. He had gone out to talk to Grandpa Catt, then walked down to the dock to look for the boat. There was no boat at the dock. That was very confusing, since he knew the boat was always there, where he tied it up and where it stayed until he went for it again. But it was missing, and so were Mr and Mrs Dandow.

'Just water, I think he's saying,' said Mum, Gideon signalling flatly with his arms and getting upset again.

Then, it seemed, he had come home, and gone down again, still looking, for some reason that puzzled Mum.

'He thought it was a dream,' said Eva. 'He gets dreams in his head as well as noises.'

The bandage bothered Eva more, but was easiest to explain. Mum had taken Gideon to the surgery and a lighter dressing had been put on his hand: since a doctor and not a nurse had tied the bandage it had come loose and untidy. Mum pulled it together and threaded a safety-pin across the palm of his hand.

Gideon being pleased with the pin, but still wanting to find the boat and set to work.

'I'll go down with him now,' said Eva. 'Then if I know it isn't there he'll know it's meant to be like that. He knows it isn't morning, doesn't he?'

He knew that, they thought. Gideon understanding, but saying 'Booey' and showing Eva the safety-pin.

'It's when you can't understand him he's most like normal,' she said.

In the end everybody set off down to the dock again, except Grandpa Catt, who was in some mood of his own with his bricklaying.

The little ones crowed to Mrs Lear, but what their bird voices said no one knew. They came to Gideon and gazed at his bandage and safety-pin, which seemed to them as important as Delfont, the stitched-up blanket.

'I think Delfont is their god,' said Eva, getting the word from their song.

'Hush,' said Mum, in case Mrs Lear heard her. 'Let's hope they don't offend anyone else of the same name.'

Mercury stuck his foot in a drain grating and began to yelp. Gideon getting impatient when Mum had to get the foot out, then the sandal, put Mercury and the sandal together, and cruelly make him walk (when she knew he could only run).

At the dock ('At last,' said Eva, and Mum said, 'Careful, fifty yards to go yet') the boat was now tied up. Mr Dandow was in it, sweeping and tidying. Mrs Dandow was in her office, typing.

Gideon striding ahead and going on board, greeting Mr Dandow cheerfully.

'Back again, then,' said Mr Dandow. 'Doing well, bist thee?'

Gideon offering his bandage and safety-pin for a handshake, and Mr Dandow giving him an elbow shake.

Gideon going up and down his boat to see that all was well and that things had been kept up while he was away.

'When is he going to be ready?' Mr Dandow asked Mum.

'Thinks he's ready now,' said Mum. 'Couldn't make it out when he came down before and the boat wasn't here.'

'He shouldn't come back if he can't do the work,' said Mr Dandow. 'My missis do dodge on and off and wind the bridges and locks.'

'He's bound to come, I think,' said Mum.

'He don't know it be work,' said Mr Dandow. 'But he be such a good boy that if was only half a boy he'd be as good. So I'll give un a word about tomorrow, see.'

Gideon happy with the boat, listening to him, copying his actions of sleeping, getting up, and coming after that. Tansy and Mercury stood beside and imitated. Gideon, not liking to be mocked, shouting 'Rauh' at them and sending them scurrying back to Mum, Mercury limping horribly, Tansy looking in the palm of her hand at an imaginary safety-pin.

Eva thought, She isn't very religious; nothing will happen like nails going through; but saints would be like Tansy and Mercury – a naughty kind of saint.

Gideon shaking hands again, coming ashore, turning Mum round and marching her off home. At home Gideon going to bed as soon as he could, then getting up and finding it was not morning after all, in spite of the routine he had put into it. Gideon going to bed again, later on, teeth cleaned ferociously.

In the morning Gideon waking and going to work before Eva got to breakfast.

When she came back he was still not home.

'Must be all right,' said Mum, 'or we'd have heard.'

Eva went out into Edenfields to see what Grandpa Catt was doing, because he was not on the scaffolding ready to come in for a cup of tea, and Mum wanted to rescue him from Tansy and Mercury, who must be with him.

Tansy and Mercury were silently watching a clump of nettles, making strange movements with their fingers.

'Quiet, we're stinging,' they said, charming the nettles ever so wisely.

Grandpa Catt was in his own garden picking currants and having a think, he said, about the brickwork. He would have his tea later.

Eva took the little ones in and half-way up the stairs to the bath.

Gideon coming in weary, and more than weary, nursing his hand, his whole arm.

'Tears down his face,' said Mum. 'What has Dandow done to him?'

Gideon weary but not unhappy; laying his arm on the table and hoping to be fed lumps of cake.

'Not so bad,' said Mum. 'Eat your own cake, Gid. But I'll have a word with Dandow.' She took Gideon's hand and tightened the dirty bandage. 'I don't know what the doctor will say about this,' she said, Gideon not caring what the words were like but relishing the attention. 'Oh my goodness, you've set it bleeding again, all seeped through it has. Well, I wonder what mischief that will be.'

Mr Dandow came in later with Grandpa Catt.

'I can't stop un,' he told Mum before she had said a word. 'He goes at it like he hadn't got any problem, and he will do all himself, winding the bridges back, taking up lock paddles, opening the gates, and nothen to be done with un but let un do it.'

'He's opened it up,' said Mum. 'Bleeding again.'

'I do know that,' said Mr Dandow. 'Why I come round. I d'wish he had the sense not to hurt himself so; but there, 'twould hurt un more not to be let do anything.'

Gideon drinking three cups of tea and falling asleep, his hand forgotten.

'Worse tomorrow,' said Mr Dandow, shaking his head.

The next day Gideon went to work, but Eva stayed at home, because it was Saturday. The day after that Gideon understood it was Sunday and that he had the day off and went nowhere in particular. Next door Mr and Mrs Lear sang particularly long hymns, but Gideon did not hear them.

CHAPTER ELEVEN

Gideon's bandage on the stairs in the mornings now.
Mum threw away the pad of dressing when it was stained;
but day by day the dressings were drier, until the same
one would do another day and another, and the last one
was lost at work. The bandage grew shorter and shorter
as Mum trimmed it down, until it was like the knot in the
corner of a handkerchief, to remind Gideon of his hand,
not for protecting it any more.

Gideon taking the remnants off to wash his hands. Eva
brought herself to look at the hand, with two fingers
missing and a slice off the side. She could not touch it
until the skin had grown again. Gideon looking at it
himself, and no one knowing what he thought.

Gideon sensing it, however, when the missing part

87

ached or moved, or felt heat. Gideon looking at it with a dumb patience.

'It's like what he hears,' said Mum. 'Just a painful noise, but there right enough.' She gave Gideon aspirin and cups of tea.

'He should stop work,' said Eva. 'Shouldn't he?' She knew that if she had been working so long on the canal, she would have learnt it all by now and tired of it.

'It isn't the work,' said Mum. 'Well, we don't know what he thinks, rightly, but working occupies his mind, like dogs want walks and herding sheep, and people can't speak to them.'

Except the little ones, thought Eva. They know.

Gideon sucking up his tea like a cow, but still feeling a pain in the lost fingers.

Eva went out at these times, when Gideon certainly did not want her, and talked to Grandpa Catt, or sometimes listened over the wall to Mr and Mrs Lear as they sang, or talked over the gate with them.

'It's like a pain,' said Mrs Lear, 'when we can't remember parts of a hymn or sacred song.'

Grandpa Catt these last few days uneasy about his building, on his ladders alone, edging into place a roof truss, levering, pulleying, levelling, the bones of the house growing out along the sky with a right and inevitable exactness, like music ending.

Before the last chords of that section the weather grew wet again, and Grandpa came down from the top of the house in the showery evening. He was discovered in the kitchen with Gideon, and both had snails crawling on their hands. Gideon using his middle word, 'Baooh', somewhere between 'Rauh' and 'Dthth'.

'They could be outside,' said Mum, firmly. 'Please.'

'It's not just snails,' said Grandpa. 'These are the kind called wallfish. They're a delicacy, and I brought you some, Daphne.'

'I couldn't come to it,' said Mum.

There were wet days after that. Grandpa Catt did no building. Eva imagined him at his house cracking the shells of snails and munching the creatures, their horns waving goodbye down his gullet.

Gideon going to work in the mornings, with his wisp of bandage on, and coming back wet and happy.

A school holiday came and moved itself along. It made no difference to anyone but Eva, and meant she did not have to get up so soon in the morning. She did not have to wake when Gideon shouted, but she did.

She woke in the depths of a rainy night at some other noise, darkness all round. She thought she heard Grandpa out on his scaffolding again, moving his tools, shifting beams, tapping at a brick to halve it, driving in a peg; or below, mixing mortar, the scrape of a shovel, the hiss of sand. There were two possibilities: either there was a ghost, working away in the rain, or Grandpa had become mad from eating wallfish.

Or a forty-foot wallfish was climbing the house.

There was a big sigh outside, and something fell heavily. The house vibrated, and then there was stillness again, only the purring of rain and the slap of water into the yard from a gutter.

The stairs light went on. Mum came through, looking in each room.

'Did you hear it?' she asked.

'It's a ghost,' said Eva, preferring that to a forty-foot snail or Grandpa Catt out of his wits.

'Open the window,' said Mum. 'We'll look from here.' She pointed Eva's bedside light into the night, putting her head out to see better. 'They've got it pretty dark out there,' she said. 'I'll go down and have a look from the front door. I think it's thieves after the wood, and if I see a lorry I'll know, because they've brought it to take it away.'

Eva sat in bed working out the meaning of that, and went to sleep until morning.

She was woken in broad daylight, with rain still falling, by the sound of Grandpa Catt walking about downstairs, mad in an angered sense, and having a continuous grumble. Eva went down to see what it was.

'Might as well build it of ice-cream,' he was saying. 'All my own fault too, and hang it, I should have known better by a long way. Well, there's no fool like an old fool, they say, and I'll say it with them. But 'tes no great problem, what went wrong. 'Tes a worse problem being an old fool.'

'Evie's just making some tea for herself,' said Mum. 'Down late because of being woken in the night.'

Eva filled the kettle and put it to boil. 'What was it?' she asked. 'I couldn't think in the night.'

'Old fool,' said Grandpa. 'Doesn't know whether a brick's been baked or not, and these hadn't, all that we got out of the hearth. Never fired, that lot. I built with raw brick, and come the rain they melted, softened, washed away, all sucked out and only the mortar left standing, and down come the roof trusses, and the whole world can see what a fool I been, what foolishness. But who would think of a brick that many years old not being a baked one, all I used, and all in the hearth yonder, all raw as eggs. And me, rawest of all, maybe addled: I mean, my roof did just now fall in.'

The little ones were skipping in their room.

'That might have done it,' said Eva. 'It sounds the same.'

'It wasn't them,' said Mum, absently, reading her letters, puzzling over them.

'I'll have some tea,' said Grandpa Catt. 'Then I'll go on top and tidy up. Fancy working away all that time and not knowing better! When the bricks ran a shade bigger, I just thought they might be metric, and took no notice.'

The little ones, in yellow coats and magic cloaks, watched the dismantling from their shop in the hearth.

Mum read her letters again. 'It's the Club again,' she said. 'I never got written back about Gideon's holiday because I suppose I thought he was too old, but he isn't and I don't suppose he ever will be, and here they are saying about the week after next, and I don't know what to reply, because I can't discuss it with him. And he's happy where he is, as good as a holiday is his work, but when he sees the bus coming he's always so glad to go, because he can remember, even if he can't foresee so much. Well, I suppose I'll try to tell him, like packing his bag up, and see whether that brings it in mind.'

Gideon going out one day and seeing the Club coach waiting to take him on holiday, expecting him to climb in. Gideon striking his head as it buzzed with noise and thought.

Gideon saying 'Dthth' to it at first, and going in and calling for 'Barbosch', then turning back and saying 'Gaboo' to the girl who was driving.

Gideon not going in for Paddington, and saying 'Voy, voy,' to himself, because he had made up his mind.

Gideon going to stand behind Mum, saying 'Baooh, baooh,' gently in a roar, so that no one took him away.

Gideon offering Mercury as a guest instead, but the coach driving off without him.

Gideon inspecting the road for some time, going up it a little way, down to the corner below Mrs Lear's house, then coming back for his sandwiches.

Gideon going to work.

'Free choice,' said Mum. 'That was right. He chose what he wanted, and he knew about them both. If he didn't know then I'd have told him. Easy, really, choosing one good thing or another.'

'You can't tell him new things,' said Eva. 'Like tomorrow and not putting your hand between the boat and the quay.'

'We can all have what we want,' said Mum.

Mercury chose worm for breakfast, which was not what Mum meant. Tansy wanted egg, so the two were cooked together, the egg nestling in Mercury's single strand of spaghetti; one boiling soft, the other hard.

Outside, Grandpa Catt dispiritedly took the house to pieces before it fell down or crumbled away. He had to be given frequent cups of tea.

Gideon coming back from the canal at the end of his

day and wanting to have the Club holiday now. The little ones stopped being Spiderman and his pet spider, Spider Spider, and went to be retired super-heroes with him.

Gideon being an uneasy retired super-hero, going to the door and looking up and down the road, fetching Paddington, waiting to say goodbye to Mum. Mum explaining that he could not go on the Club holiday just for the night. Gideon saying 'Rauh, rauh,' not wanting to believe it.

Small retired super-heroes swarmed on him and drove the holiday from his mind.

But Gideon not being quite settled at home when he went to his usual bed, and in the morning looking from the window to be sure there was nothing to distract him, like Club coaches and Gaboos.

CHAPTER TWELVE

Grandpa Catt began cutting and stacking the bundles of firewood, called faggots, going about Edenfields with a hedging hook, leaving white scars among the low trees. He chopped and chunked all day, heaping the faggots in the house-end he was building. Tansy and Mercury kept bringing the bundles out and making other houses with them. Each night Grandpa Catt carried the bundles back.

Somewhere a sweet autumn bonfire burned. Eva thought about Bonfire Night a few weeks ahead, concluding that Grandpa was preparing a big surprise for the little ones, and that she would not spoil it for them by telling them: unlike Gideon, they could understand ahead, without knowing that two months away was longer than ten minutes.

Eva's school term began. For a few days she had to drag herself from bed when she heard Gideon wake and shout. One Friday evening Mr Dandow brought Gideon home in the van. Mum jumped up alarmed in case something had gone wrong again, an injury to Gideon or the boat.

'Nothen like that,' said Mr Dandow. He stepped inside because there was a hailstorm outside. Hailstones lay in his hair.

'You get to wonder,' said Mum. 'With him. We wonder, don't we, Gid?'

'Booey,' said Gideon, settling in his chair by the fire.

'He's been a good lad,' said Mr Dandow. 'A very good lad. But the season be finished, and more.'

'Is it the end of the season?' said Mum. 'I never thought about that.'

'Why, yes, 'tes the end,' said Mr Dandow. 'I sent a letter up with his money a week since.'

'Oh, we've never seen any money,' said Mum. 'And he'll have thrown the letter away: he doesn't think any better of letters than he does of notes. I reckon we'll find the metal money at last, but not the letter. You haven't given him paper still, have you?'

'No,' said Mr Dandow. 'I remembered that, but I didn't relate it to letters. But I haven't given this week's wage.' And he pulled out a pocketful of gold, silver, bronze. 'All this,' he said, and gave a double handful to Gideon.

Gideon letting the coins fall in his lap, pushing away Tansy and Mercury, gathering the money up for himself, taking it away, while Mum did not appreciate what he was doing, and Eva did not think about it at all.

'All the passengers, like,' Mr Dandow continued to say, 'they do fancy him, and he do do marvellous well with little ones ('Doesn't do much for them at home,' said Mum), and they do say the Lord do love the cheerful, and that be Gideon. But the season's done now, and Mrs Dandow and me, well, our season be done too, and time to sell up, we reckon, so we got nothen for next year, neither.'

Then Mum was thanking Mr Dandow for having Gideon at all, and hoping she would always be so lucky in finding an understanding employer, because that was what Gideon would always need.

'Though, mind you, he had his accidents,' said Mr Dandow, going out of the door, refusing cups of tea, having his bristly hair filled again with hailstones. Hailstones were crushed again by the door as it closed.

Gideon coming in at the back door with more of them, but his hands empty.

'Where is it?' asked Mum. 'Where do you keep it, you old miser? You're not getting any more.'

'Hyagh,' said Gideon, hungry now.

Gideon on Monday feeling he had been off work long enough. He liked a change but not an alteration. Gideon getting up and wanting to go to work.

'No work,' said Mum. 'No boat. Holiday for you.' She made him sit down when he wanted to leave. She did not cut him his sandwiches. 'Pity, mind, but true. Be glad of what you had.'

Gideon saying 'Baooh' indignantly, at last realizing that Mum would not let him go out. Gideon saying 'Rauh' and banging his head behind his ear, full of noise and confusion. Gideon not able to know that a time was over; Gideon always wanting Now.

Gideon sobbing and going upstairs to bed again.

Mum, pale and trembly, said, 'All right in a while. We can't go through it for him: he has to do it all; that's where it's worse for him.'

Tansy and Mercury went to Gideon and sat on his bed, one holding a complete hand, the other a damaged one, stroking his face for him, now and then running to the bathroom for tissues to wipe his nose and mop a tear, knocking his glasses off to do it.

Mum poured herself tea with a shaky hand. Eva hastened to school, taking with her a tear down either cheek.

When she came back in the evening Gideon was busy, but he was not doing what he felt he should be doing.

Gideon tramping across Edenfields with a bundle of faggots on his back, going from house to brick-hearth. Beside him manfully strode Tansy and Mercury, like Atlas and Goliath, with a bundle each across their shoulders, patient, weary, carrying Gideon's troubles too.

'Grandpa will go mad,' said Eva.

'No,' said Mum. 'He's about to fire the kiln, the brick-hearth; that's what it's all about. There's enough brick in there to finish the job, he reckons, but lying there unfired half a lifetime.'

'There goes my bonfire,' said Eva. 'When will he do it?'

'When the boat comes in,' said Mum.

Eva thought that was some remark about Mr Dandow until she saw what a mess the kitchen was, and knew that Mum had been reading one of Dad's letters coming on the second post, and done nothing all day, apart from starting several bouts of cookery and finishing none of them.

'In a day or two,' said Mum. 'For several weeks.'

'I'll help,' said Eva.

'They can manage,' said Mum. 'They've been at it all afternoon. They're happy. As sandbags,' she added.

'I mean I'll help you, Mum,' said Eva. 'What are you trying to make?'

'Bricks, seemingly,' said Mum. 'I forgot the baking powder in the little cakes, and that's the whole of my success today.'

'Well, we're the ones in charge,' said Eva. 'While they're all working, let's get everything perfect. And sort of special for Gideon because it's not a perfect day for him and we can't do anything else.'

'But he'll eat manger and all without noticing what's in it,' said Mum.

'As well as that,' said Eva, 'if we don't get organized we shan't get anything until Dad's here, and then you'll burn it raw.'

'I know,' said Mum. 'He gets much better food on the ship, but the cook's a man, so he doesn't fancy him.'

CHAPTER THIRTEEN

Gideon waking each morning for the next ten days as usual, a shout, a tramp of feet, a thundering down the stairs.

'He hopes I'll relent and send him off to work,' said Mum. 'He thinks it's me stopping him, I know.'

Gideon giving up at last. One morning Eva woke without hearing his shout, without the quick march across the floor next door, without the avalanche down to the kitchen. That morning she woke to the sweet twittering of two pink birds putting with their soft beaks, into her sleeping mouth, worms and feathers, because she was their chick.

The chick flew into her feathers of school clothes, off the nest and down to the ground floor of the kitchen.

Here mother hen scratched about in cupboards and laid tables, she said, not eggs. 'Haven't you got plenty of time? You're always early.'

'Gideon,' said Eva. 'I didn't hear him.'

'He hasn't got up,' said Mum. 'He just looked at me and stopped moving. I think it's my fault, and I expect he feels depressed. But he always used to be up first, so I don't know why he's changed that.'

Upstairs, robbed of their child, the two little birds took worms and feathers to Gideon. Gideon waking at last, roaring at them to chase them from his room while he dressed. The little birds came down and perched on chairs. All they could say was 'Teet, teet,' and peck at cornflakes.

Gideon getting up late always now. Gideon staying out of the house as much as possible.

'He's gone off me,' said Mum. 'When I went to his room he closed the door against me.'

'Little boys do,' said Grandpa Catt. 'He's big, but still a little boy.'

'He's done it before,' said Mum. 'I know the way you mean, but this isn't that sulk. You get over that sulk in a few minutes.'

'Well then,' said Grandpa Catt, 'it isn't you, is it? It's the world; it's the way he is; it isn't your fault or doing. It's Bob Dandow ending his trips for the year and not doing them again. You want to get written to Dennis about that. Gideon has to come through his own life in his own way, hasn't he?'

'I don't know,' said Mum. 'Perhaps he just wants a kick up the grongo.'

Grandpa Catt had some success taking Gideon out on damp nights to gather wallfish, and that helped the whole day along.

Gideon leaning against the gate next door and talking to Mr and Mrs Lear. Mr Lear was good at that, even when other people might think he was asleep. If Gideon could see you, you were awake.

The doctor said it was hard to tell with Gideon, and was he eating well? After that Mum noticed that he was not eating so much and so often. 'I don't think he had great senses of choice,' she said, 'but I did think he knew one taste from another. Maybe that's gone, but I don't see how. I think he doesn't feel very special, and that's it.'

Grandpa Catt stacked the inside of the brick-hearth full with bundles of wood. 'As I remember,' he said, 'and my first work was in this brickfield, in those days we filled with wood as they filled with brick. But this last firing, it never was done, and so of course I thought it *was* fired. Maybe they put the brick in out of a sort of habit, the time they left the workings. I can't get all round the back myself, not being the size, and not being able to ply so well.

Eva wriggled in with him, and sometimes instead of him, because she could still ply, to pull the faggots round and jam them round the angles between the hearth wall and the bricks themselves. At the end of the narrow way there was darkness lit by stars of light through the brick-stack, and a strange moon lying on soot and twigs, which was the daylight dropping down the chimney, filtered and pale, thinned of its brightness. A remote wind hummed up the hollow column. A doll's teacup stood in the moony light, left by Tansy or Mercury on some un-official trip.

'We'll wait for the right breeze,' said Grandpa, 'and for your Dad, and then I'll have help disburdening when the firing's done.'

'There's more bricks than fire,' said Eva. 'If it was a pie it wouldn't cook.'

'Ah,' said Grandpa, 'bricks burn on their own, and the faggots will just make a start for that. And maybe a finish for that old chimney, I shouldn't wonder, and time it was down.'

Gideon watching all this and saying nothing. Gideon once showing a little interest when Grandpa dug in the end of Edenfields where the clay still was, and brought what he called a clow of it in the wheelbarrow to seal gaps in the structure.

Gideon was not able to wheel the barrow, with his hand tender, weak and ungainly, the weight and the pain too much for him. Gideon playing with wet clay, but not staying long at it.

'One time that would have kept him all day,' said Mum.

'It's keeping Grandpa,' said Eva.

Gideon not allowing Mum to hold his hands and see how clean they were.

Dad came back one morning when Eva was at school. She came home and found his bags lying at the foot of the stairs, but the house was empty, the kettle had a limp coldness on the stove, and the fire was a mere vegetable.

There was no one outside either. Eva came in again

and looked round for a note saying something like, 'Take a number 134 pumpkin to the ball.' There was nothing.

Nobody was upstairs. But, looking from her window, she saw smoke lifting slowly from the chimney of the brick-hearth, overflowing rather than blowing away.

She thought, They have gone down to the canal to see Mr Dandow, or I missed them at the shops.

She went out, and over to the hearth. Here the burning wood could be smelled, and the burning be heard moving slowly. There was an opening for the draught, but inside only a cold-looking ash: another vegetable fire.

Grandpa came across Edenfields from his house.

'Don't hang too close to that,' he said. 'The smoke comes out poisonous, they say. It's what you can't feel and smell that do choke you. Did they find him?'

'Who?' said Eva. 'Mercury?'

'Gideon,' said Grandpa, making it sound equally worrying. 'Just as soon as your Dad came in he walked out, and no one has seen him. I didn't know, just then, about it, so I lit my fire here. So they've gone looking. I've looked to my house, and he's not there.'

'There's no one here at all,' said Eva. 'In the house, not in Edenfields. Where are the little ones?'

'With Mrs Lear,' said Grandpa. 'Proper visiting day for her, and I don't want them underfoot, do I?'

'I'll go down to the canal,' said Eva. 'He'll be there; and if Dad goes looking that won't work, not just now. He won't be sulky with me; he doesn't mind me.'

'Right enough if he's there,' said Grandpa. 'I'll watch here.'

'I could take the little ones,' said Eva. 'He might like

that. He might not. Grandpa, do the kitchen fire, because you know, and I'll just run down and get him back and the little ones will want their tea.'

'Calm down,' said Grandpa. 'You're like your mother, everything all at once. Why don't you do the fire yourself, and stay home?'

'That isn't what happens,' said Eva. 'It isn't what I'm doing.'

She explained that she knew Gideon could not be far away, and would come back, and that she really wanted to see Dad, and he was most likely to be by the canal, and if he wasn't there he would have been there not long ago, and that would make the place different.

'I'll do the fire,' said Grandpa. 'What's one more? Gideon won't be far off: he doesn't know how to be.'

Eva went down the road in a hop and skip way, so that each footfall throbbed right through her whole body. She arrived at the quay out of breath and with her eyes bouncing.

No boat was tied up there. The water looked empty, empty, as if nothing had been in it for years. Of course it looked merely like water, if she wanted it to.

Mr Dandow's office was locked up. Behind the glass door letters had accumulated below the letter box, spreading over the floor. There was nothing here to be told, and no one to tell her it. Even the ice-cream kiosk was shut up. Nothing happened down here at this time of year.

No Gideon. No Mum and Dad; not as echo, not as memory.

She went home more slowly than she had come. At

home the fire was strong. She gave it a welcoming prod with the poker, put the kettle on, and went next door for the little ones.

'Peaceful, like,' said Mrs Lear. 'Here this morning, all the fire-irons on the hearth rug, telling Mr Lear such things. He said he knew, but there, it was like birds. Mr Lear, he understands the hens, he says, so no problem.'

'If they aren't here I won't take them,' said Eva. 'Thank you for having them. Thank you for not having them, too.'

She went home, next door, and studied the kettle while it boiled. When she drew it off the heat there was only herself. Grandpa had gone home again. She was marooned in the desert island of her own house.

She went upstairs and looked at homework. Before long there were noises downstairs, and Mum came into the house, Dad talking beside her, just a voice until she saw him.

Dad's beard a new, forgotten smell.

'He hasn't been in, then?' said Mum. 'I suppose? And the little ones.'

'Not here,' said Eva.

'Oh no,' said Mum. 'Next door.'

'Went to the canal,' said Dad. 'And the police. We'll get him back all right. It's what we do next we can't tell.'

'Find the little ones,' said Eva, and Mum gradually noticed that they were neither there, nor next door.

'Where have they taken him?' said Mum.

CHAPTER FOURTEEN

Eva was stumbling about on Dad's baggage at the bottom of the stairs. There was much more of it than usual, laying traps and springing snares.

Dad leapt over it all and went up the stairs two or three at a time, and looked in all the bedrooms. Coming down, looking at Mum, his feet finding their own neat brisk way, he said, 'Full alert, we have now. Where have they got to? There's no three less suited to be out on their own.'

Grandpa plodded into the kitchen, was looked at in case he was three other people, and then not looked at, since he wasn't.

'They weren't there,' said Eva. 'They weren't at Mrs Lear's, and we don't know where they are. You haven't got them since, have you?'

'Scarcely seen them this day,' said Grandpa. 'But come, they'll have a den they're hidden in, to Edenfields. Eva, you look with me. But, mind, I've never heard a word all day.'

'They're within walking distance,' said Dad. 'Go on, Eva, look in Edenfields. I'll run up the road and see whether they're wandering that way.'

'It'll be the canal or the river,' Mum was saying as Eva ran out of the house to traverse the paths in Edenfields, from the field fence to the claypit and round by the wall with the wood beyond, and back past Mrs Lear's house, where a pie was cooking in onion and gravy.

'One or the other,' Mum was still saying when Eva came back alone and breathless, shaking her head, and Dad was coming in at the door. The two of them were panting like dogs.

'Have to go to the telephone again,' said Dad. 'But one thing (breath) they'll be easier to spot (breath) three of them like that not just (breath) one.'

'I'll be here,' said Grandpa, 'what say; and you three go down the hill and look. That's where they'll be.'

'In the river, in the canal?' said Mum.

'No, Daph,' said Grandpa. 'Time of their lives shopping, I don't know, that crew; but not in no trouble.'

'What were they wearing?' said Dad, as they went down the hill. 'Coats?'

Eva ran back to look on the hooks. They were wearing, or had taken, yellow coats, and probably magic cloaks as well.

'Probably this minute talking,' said Dad, 'to some

bewildered constable, wanting to find the way home, but he can't understand what any of them is saying.'

Eva, walking beside him, hurrying with him, had a picture of all three being put aboard the saucer to Novendore, since they were obviously aliens. At the same time she had a tombstone vision of angels and memorials, and had to drive that from her mind by looking forward to seeing them in an instant from now, busy by the roadside.

Now, and now, and now went by. Then they were at the bottom of the hill and looking at the quayside again.

'Boat gone,' said Mum. 'Dandow must have sold it.'

'Oh, well then,' said Dad. 'Be up the shops, I reckon,' and he wanted to go on past the entrance to the quay and look at the little group of Post Office and supermarket and butcher. Mum made him go on to the quay and down to the far end, where the water went out to the canal.

The water there lay as it did in the basin, still but not inert, with ripples opening and closing and echoing faint from the bank, looking one way dark, the other light.

Mum looking for yellow coats afloat.

'Of course not,' said Dad; but Eva could tell he had been tensely waiting to jump into the water until he had seen nothing there.

Coming out from the quay into the road again they had to step aside to let Mr Dandow's van come through. He gave them a look and a nod, to Mum and Eva, then a stare, which was towards Dad. He stopped the van immediately, and got out.

'I just come down for the letters and that,' he said. 'But you'll be wanting a talk, eh?'

'Not just now,' said Dad. 'I've been back hardly a minute, really, and we've lost Gideon.'

'Gidden do know his way about,' said Mr Dandow. 'I can tell 'ee.'

'Those little ones are off with him,' said Mum. 'This long time.'

'Oh my dear,' said Mr Dandow. 'But they'm just lost, not comen to any harm, like being with a big dog, with Gidden, but can't find his way home if he isn't arrived to a place he do know.'

'But still,' said Mum, 'that set. That lot.'

'Sick with worry, she is,' said Dad. 'We'd best go on and telephone the police again.'

'Right enough,' said Mr Dandow. 'But let me get the van turned about and pick up my letters, and come up the house and telephone from there, or better still, go up the station and you'll be nearest what's going on. I'll just run you up, eh?'

His head moved about in the shadows inside the van, so flat up the sides it was like a block of unreflective mirror, changing the light but not showing pictures.

He drove on to the quay and turned the van round, got out, opened the office door, and scooped up the mail that had come for him, and slammed the door shut again.

Instead of getting into the van he walked to the front of it, shedding his letters as he came, gazing out at the water, not at where he was going.

Then he put the rest of the letters on the bonnet of the

van, and with his arms straight down beside him, opened his mouth, once, twice, and at a third time spoke.

'Where's my bloody boat to?' he said.

CHAPTER FIFTEEN

'I don't know where your boat is,' said Dad. 'But it seems
we should all go sharpish up to the nick and tell them
that as well.'

'Can't be far away,' said Mr Dandow. 'I haven't been
down in better than a week, but still, 'tesn't time, 'tes
distance. Too wide for the Kennet, but might be up
Gloucester way, Birmingham, paddling about the Hum-
ber, wouldn't care to cross into Holland, but folk do
do it, and once there 'tes an easy run into the Black
Sea. Rooshians,' he said. 'And I'd other ideas for it,
Dennis.'

He was picking up his letters as he spoke, stacking
them into one crooked elbow and dropping them
through, so that no progress was being made. Only Mum

moved, and she hopped from side to side, until Dad gave her a nudge to stop the twitch.

'Does he know how to start up the engine?' she said at last.

'He'd have had to,' said Mr Dandow. 'Why, who is it?'

'I mean Gideon,' said Mum, because it was clear to her that Mr Dandow was talking about a boat-thief: even if Gideon had done it, then he was not capable of stealing.

Mr Dandow was still not able to put two ideas together. 'He'd never get to Gloucester,' he said. 'That's a sea passage and no end of tides, and he wouldn't know how to begin, not Gidden. But he could start the motor, and cast off, and get along the canal. But,' and he dropped all the letters again with the thought that had come to him.

'But what?' said Dad, not allowing Mum to speak.

'Nothen,' said Mr Dandow, but he sucked in his breath and shook his head while he said so, and while he thought of the thing he was not saying.

'I wouldn't go in the river section,' he said. 'Through the lock into the old river. Not when the rain's been like it has, tippling down. There's just a time when that old river do look calm and smooth, when the tide do back up full, but when it drops and you're on the river you'll be pulled down into the docks, and out and through, and be scooted over to Wales. Well, I do hope nothen of that, none of it.'

'Could Gideon do that?' asked Dad. 'Locks and that?'

'Easy,' said Mr Dandow. 'Master of that, right enough. Sell 'un with the boat, if I could.'

'Where will they be?' said Dad. 'Let's be there.'

Mr Dandow had now gathered up most of his letters.

He slowly took them back into the office and dropped them on the desk. Then he opened a drawer and started looking for something. Mum was getting into the van, and getting out again.

Dad was waiting patiently. He had understood what Mr Dandow was doing.

'Table in here,' Mr Dandow was saying, calling out through the door.

Desk, thought Eva. Desk with typewriter.

'Tide tables,' said Dad.

'Just going down,' said Mr Dandow, bringing a sheet of paper out of the office with him, slamming the door again, giving the paper to Dad. 'Half an hour early of Sharpness.'

Instead of getting in the van he ran to the edge of the canal and looked either way. Down the water someone blew a car horn, stuck at a bridge still open and lodged at the far side.

'That's it,' said Mr Dandow. 'Left the bridges open, and I thought he was a better boy than that.'

He came back and got into the van, starting the motor. The gear stick shook its head and chattered. Dad climbed into the back, and Eva with him.

'We'll go down the Feeder road,' said Mr Dandow, 'run by the water for a mile or two, and see where they are.'

'The police could get there first,' said Mum. 'There's more of them. Ooh.' The Ooh was a big lump in the road, because Mr Dandow had taken a short cut on the way up the hill beyond the shops, crossing a building site. Muddy waters sprayed the van, and steam came up through the floor in the back.

'Stop on the bridge,' said Mr Dandow. 'You look up left, Dennis, I'll cross the road and look downstream and put an eye under the bridge too. 'Tes wide enough to hide the boat.'

Traffic built up behind them, because the van blocked that side of the road. It stood on the other side of the road too, because Mr Dandow had left his door open, and was sprawling across the parapet of the bridge, and no one dared drive through.

They went on, because there was no sign of the boat.

'Don't expect it,' said Mr Dandow. 'You can about see this bridge from the quay.'

There was a right turn under the bows of an articulated truck, which blew a foghorn at them. The van came into the potholes of the Feeder road, with water to either side, a rusty place where no one came.

The canal was slack and empty of boats. Eva wondered what the tide could do to it, because she knew, from something she had read or heard, that the canal was always exactly so full. Now it was not only at that fullness (and emptiness), but, she thought, the surface could not have settled so undisturbed in less than a day.

The van stopped where the Feeder road came out on to another dockside access. The canal went on beyond, but with only a narrow towpath.

'I'll have to go round,' said Mr Dandow. 'Half a mile the canal goes without the road, round under Shire Castle by the cliffs, getting near the river, see, that's river cliffs. She might be down there, I hope, not yet into the river.'

Dad and Eva got out. 'I'll go on,' said Mum.

'Over the fence and down through under the bridge,'

said Mr Dandow. 'I'll bring the van down by the water at yon end.' He switched on the lamps of the van, and Eva saw that all the shadows of the landscape had grown indistinct and merged with each other, because twilight was arriving.

Juicy yellow light fell from bright yellow lamps hung among houses and factories, and below them the tail lamps of cars and lorries careered like red beetles.

'Just jog,' said Dad, holding the wire down for Eva. It touched her hand, cold and set like ice.

They ran on grey ground. The canal now lay like a smooth road beside them, being pulled slowly round the curve of Shire Castle, curved itself, and empty yard by yard.

'I must get to know this part of town,' said Dad.

'(Breath),' said Eva.

There was a black lump in the water ahead, close against the bank. It was a barge, but not Mr Dandow's boat. It lay like Noah's Ark, rounded at each end, cabined or built up all along, and black as coming night.

'No one there,' said Dad, not slowing down, but giving the side a thump as he passed. No one stirred or came. Looking back when they had passed it there was no creation of ripples from its black side free in the water.

Something began to disturb the surface of the canal. There was still direct light from the sky, reflected light from warehouse windows, and the indirect light from street lamps. One, or two, or all three, illuminated a thready stretching of the skin of the water, as if it were growing small, short muscles, as if it were eddying and being sucked down, without forming whirlpools like most eddies. It was as if the air in the water had been pulled out, tightening it in on itself, to places and parts below with a fine structure of their own.

'Moving water,' said Dad. 'You see that when the tide drops down some of the big rivers, as if the water turned to sand; and then there is sand. This water is running out.'

He ran faster, a quick jog.

There was a canal end. Something lay across the lane the water made, interrupting it. It was not the boat, but lock gates that seemed to be closed.

They were not entirely closed, nor were the gates at the far end of the lock. Water ran out of the canal, being pulled through by the river beyond. There was a great deal of noise, because there was a weir across the river, at the level of the lock, to regulate the depth below. Water lashed over it, yellow even in the complete grey light. The river went on below, busy, surging, too rough and ugly to have been walked on if it were dry land.

Dad and Eva had come to the end of the place where river and canal joined, and the ground ended in a built-up point of stone with a post on it and a sign they could not read from the back, since it showed to the water.

They had no interest in the sign, but had to cross the canal. Dad went out on to a lock gate and found it firm but not closed well. He got to the wheel and closed the gates, but the water still pressed strongly through. He came back and lowered the paddles in the gates themselves, and the water filled and slowed, but still swirled.

Eva followed him across. They were on a quayside,

and the canal towpath now followed the river. Dad looked back and saw that they should have crossed higher up, below the black barge, where a bridge bowed over.

Down the towpath headlamps flashed, and there carried over the noise of the water a salute or summons on the horn of the van.

Eva knew she had seen all this in daylight from the cabin of the boat, on Gideon's first trip. But then there had been no rushing water, no coils and swipes of foam, no clamour in the throat of the river.

Dad waved towards the van. Mr Dandow seemed to catch the gesture, and the van turned away from them, the headlamps now dropping their cone of light across the river, putting eyebrows on buildings opposite, and those bright blemishes lifted from the water.

They shone on something moving in the water. The SHIRE CASTLE was there, in the middle of the flood, Gideon sitting atop, where Mr Dandow would con the helm. Down in its cabin the little lights glowed among the bottles of the bar, and jumping about on the seats were two fair-haired children, one curly, one straight, in yellow coats.

CHAPTER SIXTEEN

Gideon ahoy!

Gideon sailing his own ship. Gideon having been down the river and now coming up it, but slowly, slowly. The engine beating heavily, the boat slipping back and slipping back.

'Gideon,' shouted Mum, as Dad and Eva came up to her. 'Gid.'

Dad put his hand on her arm, and she turned and held it.

'Don't distract him,' Dad said. 'What's he done?' he asked Mr Dandow. He had to shout, or call loudly.

'He wouldn't hear me,' said Mum. 'I just wanted him to know I was here. Are they all right?'

'He's been down and turned about,' said Mr Dandow.

'No trouble there. But he can't work up the current, so he'll go down stern first out of control, so what'll we do?'

'Swim out,' said Dad.

'Never get up the side,' said Mr Dandow. 'Now, we'd best get on the pipe bridge, for he'll be back under it in a minute. Just a question of getting on the bridge first.'

The pipe bridge carried huge pipes like drains or water-mains, grey or very light in colour. From close to the light one was yellow and labelled ETHYLENE, and a black one was blue.

No one was meant to cross the bridge, or be on it. It had gates at either end, coiled wire beside its abutments and spikes over the gates.

'Make a back,' said Dad, and Mr Dandow leaned himself over, firm as the bridge itself. Dad ran up to him, kicked off, so that Mr Dandow puffed like a wounded mountain, and was up among the wired girders, in and out, suddenly free on the deck itself.

'Sailorman,' said Mr Dandow, rubbing his back. 'Jump on first thing, at the stern, and at the bow you'll find a rope coiled, no, wait a minute, maybe I can do better . . .'

Eva was at that moment wanting to remind him about a coil of rope she had been sitting on in the van, and Dad had it in mind too, so Eva was running for it before it was mentioned. Mr Dandow gave an end to Dad.

'Pay it out,' said Dad. 'Go upstream a bit. Look, I'll get well above and maybe beyond the boat and drop down, and if I miss, the rope will drop over.'

'Right,' said Mr Dandow, 'and a coil in the bows, the long one, the end's made fast, and between them we'll hold her and bring her to the bank.'

Dad shouted something else, but it was lost in the rush of the water and the putter of the engine.

The boat stopped making headway against the water. Until now it had gone up the passing flood, and stayed pointing in the right direction, upstream. Now it went slower and slower itself, and the water began to pull it down, and to turn it round.

'Be broadside on,' said Mr Dandow. 'It'll fetch up sunk.'

'Gideon's stopped steering,' said Eva. 'He's got tired of sitting there, so he's stood up and scratching his bottom and yawning.'

'He'll be hungry,' said Mum.

'So long as he isn't thirsty,' said Mr Dandow. 'With my boat along.'

Dad shifting about on the bridge, tying the rope round himself in some easy-loose knot, looking for the place to be for dropping on board.

Gideon sitting down again and the boat straightening. He had let everything go for a minute, while he had a scratch.

Dad shifted on the bridge again, because for another minute the boat made headway against the stream.

Mercury came up to the hatch to call to Gideon, and the boat yawed once more.

'I should have locked the damn thing,' said Mr Dandow.

Here we are in the middle of the city, thought Eva, and no one knows we are here, no one has seen us, and no one is even in sight. This is all quite private until they are all drowned. If they aren't I shall never send them to

Novendore. In fact, I shan't even speak to them again because of the pain they are giving me in my chest, at my heart, through my throat.

She did not see Dad jump. He was no longer there. She did not see where he had landed. She saw him getting up, standing on the roof of the boat. She saw Gideon stand up too, leaving the tiller, leaving the throttle, waving his arms, giving some sort of greeting.

The boat swung completely across the current. Gideon sat down. The little ones in the cabin fell over. The light went out.

'Lord, we might just get the one out,' said Mr Dandow. 'We don't know whenabouts to pull; I daren't tighten.'

Eva saw him standing there with the doors of his eyelids flat over his flatscreen eyes, seeing nothing, getting all his sensation through a slack rope end.

Eva got the rope herself. Mum was transfixed by the act of looking. Eva looked too, but to see what was happening. Mum was merely watching for events. Eva waited for a signal.

Dad clambering, but the boat lying over to one side, so that he had to move as on a roof. Then he was at the bow, and using his hands, his arms, and then holding them above his head.

All at once he was in the water himself, knocking his way through it towards the bank.

Mum was having a scream.

'Give up,' said Eva. 'Pull on this,' and she got rope into Mum's hand.

Dad was very heavy, she found. She thought it must

be Dad on the far end. Mr Dandow began to pull too, absorbing the ropelength like negative matter.

'He got it on,' said Mr Dandow. 'Where is he? We'll never get her round, shall we?'

Dad was climbing a ladder out of the water, a rope round his waist. He had tied the rope he took direct to the boat, very smartly, and tied the boat's rope to himself, bringing that ashore too. He moved along the towpath to a post, and took a turn of the rope round that.

'She'll pull round on that,' he said. 'Look, her stern's dropping downstream, and she should come up when she's straight.'

'You don't know the old pig,' said Mr Dandow. 'But she might. What's that boy doing?'

'Driving again,' said Eva, the only one with a spare eye.

The lights glimmered, flickered, and snapped on. Gideon at the helm sailing on.

Blue lights began to flash. Eva thought that something had climbed out of the river-bed, as it did in Novendore, making hollow shadows on all the walls. A police car grated to a halt on the cindery ground, and some questioning voices were heard.

'Just pull this,' said Mr Dandow. 'Boatload of children and, well, children.'

The boat came up the river, steady and steadier, gathering movement, closer and closer to the side.

Mr Dandow let go of the rope. 'Keep her tight and gentle,' he said. 'I'll go on board and the bottom gate of the lock is open, near as anything, so we'll go in there, and that's home, once we get out the other side into the cut.'

Gideon jumping ashore himself at the lock, swinging the gates wide, coming aboard again and bringing the boat into the lock, shutting the gates, opening the other end, able to manage it all.

The police car had gone long before the proceedings were over, the policemen disappointed that there was nothing more dramatic, flashing light over the river, hoping perhaps to collar a submarine.

'Right then, thank you,' said Mr Dandow, when the boat was in the canal and he had tied it up, and he was dismissing Gideon.

Gideon shaking hands, and going with him to the van and getting in. Mum went with them. Gideon saying 'Hyagh' very hopefully. Gideon taking Mum away from Dad.

Dad and Eva took the boat home. Dad wore a blanket instead of his shirt, and it was like being driven home by Robinson Crusoe, or perhaps Delfont. The little ones still played down below, with no idea that anything had almost happened, coming up from time to time to ask for tea. Eva went down and made sure they could not drink anything colourful from the bar.

The full darkness of night was on them when they came to the quayside. Mr Dandow was there waiting for them, tying the boat up, padlocking a shackle or two, bolting down the doors hard, taking a piece of engine away.

'Mrs Dandow, she've left home by now,' he said.

'I'll be down to see you,' said Dad. 'Come on, you two little ones.'

They went home, with a lot of tears, because one little one was too tired to walk and the other too tired to be carried, and they wanted home brought to them.

When they got home, stained and sobbing, they went into a bath.

Gideon, by the fire, drinking tea, his day's work done. Gideon in his own place.

Gideon walking out into the night when Dad came in, out into Edenfields.

'Well, I'll have to settle that,' said Dad, quite without any sense that he was going to do it now. He went up to change all his clothes, then came down and had his tea.

Gideon prowling about the yard at the back, eating the food Eva took him. Gideon not coming in, not speaking to Mum, not looking at Dad. Gideon telling Grandpa – who was shyly waiting for the right time to come in and ask what had happened – Gideon telling him that 'Rauh' was the word.

'I'll leave the door open,' said Mum. 'It's all we can do.'

'Reckon to settle it all soon,' said Dad. 'He's bad at first and always was, but you'll see.'

CHAPTER SEVENTEEN

Tansy insisting on worm because it was her turn, though she did not like it.

Grandpa Catt came in, anxious not to be intrusive.

'Gideon out there?' said Mum. 'What's he doing?'

'Maundering about,' said Grandpa. 'We'll have to wait for him to come out of it. Where did you find them to? Did you have a word with Bob Dandow?'

'You haven't heard a thing,' said Dad, and told Grandpa, who said Oh my God and Did he now?, like a prayer.

Mum listened and put a spoonful of egg in Mercury's ear. Mercury folded up a piece of bread and butter and put it in the tiny pocket of his pyjamas. Tansy filled her lap with crusts and let the worm slither to the floor.

Grandpa went out again. Mum put the little ones to bed. Eva looked from the back door and thought she saw Gideon and Grandpa at the brick-hearth, Grandpa with a torch looking for escaping smoke, Gideon with clay from the wheelbarrow.

A policeman came to the door, wanting to be sure that the event of Gideon missing and the finding of the boat were the same thing. He came inside, smelling of offices and cars and the inside of hats.

'Where is he?' he said at last. Wanting to tie up all the loose ends, Eva thought, picking the worm from the floor and dropping it into the fire.

She went to find Gideon in the dark yard, in dark Edenfields.

'Not here,' said Grandpa. 'He went in the house.'

He was not in his room. That was empty when Eva looked. She came downstairs again wondering why it had felt so extremely empty without feeling extremely sad. When Gideon was in hospital the room had been quite hollow, which is far more than being positively hollow.

Half-way down the stairs she thought she knew. She went up again to make certain.

Paddington was not there. Gideon had come in and taken Barbosch, and there was meaning in that act.

'He's gone,' she said, when she arrived at the policeman again. 'He's taken his best thing so he must be going.'

'Where now?' said Mum. 'He's tried the boat.'

'Hospital,' said Eva. 'That's where he last went with Barbosch. Paddington.'

There was some confusion about where the hospital

was and who was Barbosch and who and where Paddington might be.

'We'd better take a look outside,' said the policeman, getting his official torch.

Half an hour later he went to his car through the side gate, and switched messages to and fro on the radio. Then he went away.

Outside, Grandpa Catt and Dad talked and walked in Edenfields. At the edge of Eva's sleep an owl flew and called. Thinking it was Gideon waking she started up, but only darkness poured round her, a sinking current at the lock gate of dreams. There was silence from one next room. From the other two little snug pink pigs gruntedly sucked their sleeping thumbs in rhythm.

Gideon gone; Barbosch gone.

In the morning she woke with a twitch and a start, her mind full of a dream she had found earlier in the night, coming back to her when she woke as if she dreamed it now, by daylight, rather than remembered it. A dream of bending, plying her way past the bricks in the hearth, along those small runs where Mercury and Tansy could simply go, where Gideon might have struggled, and been walled up with the bundles of wood, sealed in with daubs of clay.

But it could not be so, because all that was done. It was a thought her mind had made the day before and only now produced, hanging there so that she heard through it, saw through it, and tasted through it.

The taste was real. The baking fume of the hearth had settled deep on the air, a smoked mist over Edenfields, a taint and trace in the whole house.

Mum was sunk in bed asleep. Dad was downstairs and touching the kitchen fire.

Gideon's room empty of him, but Mooli and Delfont poised on his pillow with crusts to eat.

Downstairs Dad blinked at her.

'Did you stay awake all night?' she asked.

'Easy job for a sailor,' said Dad. 'Some of it inside, some outside, going about wanting to call his name, as if he could hear; and it's me he doesn't want to hear or see.'

'It's both of you,' said Eva. 'He's gone off Mum because he thinks she won't let him go to work, so it's been a big sulk of his. And he's off you worse than ever because he thinks that what he thinks about Mum is what you should think too, so you haven't to like her. He's just got lost again, twice in one day.'

'He wouldn't know where to go,' said Dad. 'He knew the boat, but he can't get into that now. But he doesn't know there are places. But he could have got on a bus and be in Birmingham, he wouldn't know; and they're not looking for him there, so they won't tell him. I don't know. We'll have to wait.'

Mercury and Tansy came downstairs and began making toast in a corner of the kitchen with building blocks, spreading the butter with a sandal. Or perhaps it was mortar.

Grandpa was out in Edenfields, in weather haunted by rain that followed the mist. Where the rain walked on the hearth the mist rose, the ghost of a ghost. Grandpa crouched at the door and modified the draught by sealing with clay.

The little ones had real toast for breakfast, at last. They

reserved some, to use later in a game. The game seemed to consist of going out, in yellow coats, to Edenfields and calling for Gideon.

They sort of don't remember, thought Eva, going out after them to keep them away from the hearth. They must have been told to keep away from it, she was sure. But it was not possible to tell what they chose to remember. Poisoned vapours would not care about memory.

They had remembered, but had found a way to deal with that. They went by a devious route, against the fence, through unknown thickets, to the back of the hearth, behind the chimney stack.

Eva caught up with them there. The dry heat of the bricks bit at her throat, the wood burnt beyond wood, the substance of the brick itself burning, the harsh steam from the rain corroding her throat.

The little ones were still calling for Gideon as if they knew where he was.

This is absurd, thought Eva. They are mad and tiresome, and I'll take them home, and they will cry.

'Time to go,' she said, taking a yellow arm of each.

'We're finding Gideon,' they said, unexcitedly. They knew it was a plain fact.

'He isn't here,' said Eva. 'He's got lost, poor Gideon.'

'Poor Gideon,' they said. 'Our cloaks.'

'Why did he have your magic cloaks?' asked Eva.

They did not reply, because they had already told her the answer: Gideon had their magic cloaks, which was a good enough answer about why he had them.

Besides, they knew where the cloaks were, and Gideon. It was one of those places all three of them could identify.

'The shop,' said Tansy.

'The magic shop,' said Mercury. It was quite familiar to them, and certainly in their view not part of the hearth.

Gideon was snugged in under an overhang made by the chimney, on the ground, covered with two magic cloaks, and in some sort of sleep.

'He told us when we went to bed,' said Mercury.

'We bringed his breakfast,' said Tansy.

Then they gabbled to him. But he did not wake.

He was more than asleep; limp, insensible, without consciousness, dried and anaesthetized by the gases melting from the brick, breathed now through pale lips, his eyes closed, the lids and lenses of his glasses covered in baked dust.

Eva pulled at him, dragging him from the hollow in the ground into grass still damp.

'Get Grandpa Catt,' she said, sharply and urgently, to Mercury. 'Get Dad.'

Mercury laid his offering of burnt toast carefully on Gideon's chest and ran back towards the house.

In a little while, Gideon lying in the rain, breathing with a rattle and a sigh. Grandpa and Dad lifting and carrying him. Mum running out in her dressing-gown, unable to find her boots.

The little ones, their duty done, their cloaks recovered from Gideon's legs, were Snoopy and the Red Baron, flying among the tree clouds of Edenfields.

Eva went back to the magic shop, found Barbosch, and brought him in.

CHAPTER EIGHTEEN

'Then the one we've found can't be yours,' said the policeman. He had come round the end of the houses while Gideon was being carried indoors. Mum explained, or said things, holding Gideon's head up, its pale eyelids closed.

Tansy and Mercury jumped up at the policeman like puppies.

'Accident?' he asked, stepping aside and letting the puppies collide. They sat in the wet grass and howled.

Both of them being ignored.

'We don't know what,' said Dad.

'Doctor,' said Mum. 'Doctor first. We'll get her.'

The policeman stepped over the two little ones wrecked on the ground, and went away. Eva wondered whether things were going on, or just going. She picked up the cross victims, and they recovered enough to want to carry her in shapeless as Gideon, a new idea for them. Eva marched them indoors and dressed them, which no one had done so far.

Before she finished, Gideon was in and upstairs too, lying on his bed, Mum washing his face, Grandpa Catt going off down the stairs again for the doctor, going out of the front door as if it were his own.

'Down to the kitchen,' said Mum, coming to Eva and the little ones on the landing. 'Troop down.' Behind her Gideon's room was more vacant than ever.

At the top of the road a siren yelped and a blue light flashed in Eva's mind.

Seconds later the light flashed at the kitchen window, blue on the plates, green on the yellow walls, and sleek windows stood outside the kitchen window like an aeroplane suddenly landed and modern against the house. A V O N was written on the net curtain – the lipstick lady coming to call?

Mum would not let the ambulance men in. The thing outside began to blush with amber lights flashing round its neck. It began to speak through its nose, as if it had noises in its head like Gideon, and spoke the same gargled buzzing.

The stretcher went back into its place. Mum let the men in and they shouldered their way up the stairs, their weight moving the wood of the landing floor overhead.

In the road the ambulance spoke to itself. Mrs Lear came out of her house and stood in the road, looking up and down, in her apron. She went indoors again.

Eva sat against the fire and prodded it with the poker. The poker was cold, but the heat of the fire came through the air and penetrated her knuckles. She broke tarry blisters on the coal and a flowery gas spurted into the room. She tasted it on the air, among the flashing light from outside.

I am just myself, she thought. It is not enough. And she noticed for the first time that she had sides to her fingers as well as backs and fronts, and felt no better for it, because new facts were of no use or comfort.

The doctor and Grandpa Catt came next, swooping up the hill in a green Ford Sierra with a gold coach-line. Grandpa shook the front door, and Eva opened it. Grandpa led the way upstairs, the doctor smelling of that scentless scent medical.

Eva's instinct told her to put the kettle on. Upstairs nothing happened. Feet moved slightly. A sort of calm set in. Eva felt that her mind could pretend it was a Saturday afternoon, with nothing going on. Her mind could do it, but not herself, not her knowledge of reality.

The quiet party upstairs began to break up. First down were the ambulance men, with Dad fumbling the door open for them, exchanging words with them but not listening to what they were saying, or to what he said himself. Outside, the ambulance sulkily shut off all its lights, and slunk away down the hill. Real light came into the kitchen.

'Ah, kettle,' said Dad. 'Good girl.'

'What does the doctor say?' asked Eva. 'She knows.'

'Hasn't said it all yet,' said Dad. But then the doctor began to come down the stairs, with Mum behind her. Upstairs Grandpa Catt settled into Gideon's cane chair. The chair creaking. Gideon never having known that.

'As well here as anywhere,' said the doctor. 'You'll be able to tell whether there's any change for the worse, and let me know.' Saying it, she was out of the door and the green Sierra gone.

'What did she say in the end?' asked Eva. 'Before the last.'

'You heard her,' said Mum. 'As well here as anywhere. It's the same as saying as badly here as anywhere. Oh my God, is this when it happens, like they've said?'

'But what will happen?' said Eva, instead of screaming and knowing, looking towards the little ones who perhaps ought not to hear the answer. They were away on a magic doormat. Eva wanted knowledge, fact, certainty; something to ply, to twist.

Mum was still speaking. 'Whatever will happen will happen. You don't know a good result from a bad one. You know he can be happy or sad, and his sad is worse and his happy is less. So we don't know what's best for him, living or dying.' At that point Eva put her arms round Mum and squeezed, partly to share with her the feelings she could not express, and partly to stop the words.

Mum took her arms and held them open. 'But whatever it is,' she said, 'he's going to do it at home.'

'Nature taking its course,' said Dad. 'There's enough of us to share it, and one touch of nature makes the whole world kin.'

Then he held Mum, and Eva went upstairs to see

Gideon curled on his side, breathing so that she could hear him.

'He made more noise than this the night he was born,' said Grandpa Catt. 'And I heard him in the night, snoring like this. Thought he was that old bawson lives up in the tumps – old badger – snuffling.'

'Is he going to die?' asked Eva. 'Today? When he's not even awake?'

'I think it's up to him,' said Grandpa. 'We have to live with it, that's all.'

Eva picked up Paddington from under the bed and put him in Gideon's arms.

Gideon, sleeping; more complete.

'Barbosch,' she said. Gideon not hearing, as usual, not noticing at all.

Eva pushed her face against Grandpa's jacket. Woodsmoke came into her eyes and made her sniff. Grandpa put his hand on the roundness of the back of her head.

'My face doesn't know what to do,' she said. 'I don't know what's happening.'

She went to her room and disciplined her slightly runny nose with a tissue, washed her face, and went down to see what happened next.

In the rest of the morning nothing happened. Grandpa Catt came down and went to the brick-hearth, because this was the only firing there could be.

The little ones went up from time to time and looked at Gideon. They recovered Mooli and Delfont and laid them at his feet, face down, embracing him.

Mr Dandow came inquiring, but did not come into the house.

135

'I'll have to see you, Bob,' said Dad. 'But not just now,' and he shook his head.

Mrs Lear, not wanting to interfere, came into the road again, looking up and down, wanting to know. Dad sent Eva out to tell her, and she took the little ones with her.

Mrs Lear said she had buried one, if that was what it was come to, and that Gideon would go straight up, never fear. 'It is in the heart,' ꜱne said, 'not in the head, is wisdom – he must have that.'

It's all they think, thought Eva. She said, 'Everybody is killing him, and that isn't right. It's wanting it, wishing it.'

'They can have their dinner with us,' said Mrs Lear, after a small pause, without contradicting Eva. 'That will be good.' Eva realized that she was furious and had insulted Mrs Lear and made her angry.

'I don't want him to, that's all,' she said.

'It's a different thing,' said Mrs Lear. 'Indeed.'

'Safe in the arms of Jesus,' sang Mercury.

'There's room in thy heart for me,' carolled Tansy.

They were being insensitively angelic, Eva decided, and left them.

'Good,' said Mum, when she was back home.

Eva had her meal in an acute state of emergency, with nothing emerging. With Gideon upstairs, not quite a being, she did not herself exist. Mum stayed upstairs and drank a pot of tea, and tried to eat a round of toasted cheese without being able to chew it damp enough to swallow.

Every time she saw Gideon lying there, she curled up

inside, she said, like the pain of giving birth to him all over again.

'That's what Grandpa was saying,' said Eva.

'You get the same feeling,' said Dad. 'Something's due, but we don't know what.'

Tansy and Mercury came back, with their verse of sacred song. The song was unbearable to Mum, until she laughed it devoid of meaning.

It is a prayer, thought Eva. They are now angelically sensitive.

Gideon snoring gently.

CHAPTER NINETEEN

Gideon lying in bed the next day. Eva saw him as she went down in the morning, a mound under the counterpane, his hair showing on the pillow. Soft toys on the floor under the bed like detached parts of him.

All there is now, she thought.

Mum had stayed by the kitchen fire all night, and breakfast was ready.

'I'm all right,' said Mum. 'It gives me something to do.' She clattered the kettle against the tap.

There are worse noises in her head, Eva thought: noises like Gideon's, noises no one else can hear. Eva wished she could absorb some of that noise herself, but all she heard was the clarity of actual day; all she felt was pain actual in her chin and the sides of her face.

'When you go,' said Mum, 'wake Dad up. I sent him to bed. And don't be late for school; and,' when Eva replied in very quiet tones, 'don't let's whisper to each other.'

'It's not normal,' said Eva. 'What else can we do?'

'It's normal for what it is,' said Mum.

The little ones, on their way down after a subdued waking, went in to Gideon and replaced Mooli and Delfont by his knees. They came downstairs in single steady quiet, not mob-footed as on other days.

'Only morning,' said Eva to Dad, when she looked in on him and he woke startled, ready to climb the mizzen mast or cope with Mum's weather or Gideon's full tide of sleep ebbed out.

'Tell her I'm coming down,' he said, moving a drooping and sleepy hand towards a shirt. He was asleep again before Eva was out of the room.

At school she was shouted at for looking out of the window all the time, though it was not the outside but the distant inside she stared into.

At home there was a smell of disinfectant. In the road was the green Ford Sierra, and in the house the doctor, coming down the stairs as Eva opened the back door. Eva heard her talking to Mum and Dad. Next door Tansy and Mercury were talking loudly to Mr and Mrs Lear.

The front door closed. The disinfectant stayed: Mum making the whole house a sickbay.

Mum herself looking ill. 'She said you were a patient now too,' said Dad. 'You have a sleep, Daph. Evie and I can look after things.'

'There's nothing to look after,' said Mum. 'So I might as well stay awake.'

Dad, however, saw her up to bed and came back to the kitchen.

'It's the same as it was with him,' he said. 'No change.'

'I'll go up and look before I do my homework,' said Eva. I'm planning to visit a well-known scene, she thought. Barbosch, Mooli and Delfont were on a chair. She put them back on watch on the bed. There was a single tear in the corner of Gideon's eye. The curtains of the window were half drawn across. Everything is never the same, she thought. Gideon breathing privately.

In Edenfields Grandpa Catt was moving things about by wheelbarrow.

'I'll be outside,' said Dad. 'Grandpa is getting bricks, unburdening the hearth, and I'm helping. Shout if you need me.'

Eva sat at the kitchen table and daylight sleep filled the house. Even the fire had nothing to say. Only from outside came the scraping chink of brick being lifted and tipped, dry as sugar under a foot.

Gideon's sleep filling the house, making it as it was; Mum's sleep being the strange one: one was a broken ship, the other had no one at the wheel.

Later on there was knocking at the door. Two doctors were on the step, and in the road a black Jaguar and the green Sierra.

There was walking about upstairs, and walking down again, talking at the bottom of the stairs.

'. . . Hospital perhaps . . .' said a man.

And Mum, more clearly than usual, more firm, knowing better than usual: 'If he lives he bears it; if he doesn't, I bear it, and I can do it better.'

Dad saying something about Nature's way. And the door closing.

'They're in another world,' said Mum, coming into the kitchen, in her hand a silvery card with little pills pressed into it. She looked at it for a moment, then put it carefully on the back of the fire. 'I don't want that. I'm not anxious. If I eat them I shan't know anything. A different world, and they think you want a chemical if you ever get a real feeling. It's hell, but I'm not anxious.'

'But they understood,' said Dad.

'When *they* understand *they* don't need pills,' said Mum. 'And when *I* understand *I* don't need them either,' and she stirred the card down into the fire, where the heat rotted it without burning it decently.

Eva stared at Mum and Dad, wishing a draught was not attacking her eyes, that her nose was not getting warm.

Dad came across and held her hands. 'That was a brain doctor,' he said. 'Of course it's a different world for them. But we all agree that if Gideon . . . falls asleep now, well, that's the way it has to be; we don't argue with what has to happen.'

'If he wakes up, well and good,' said Mum. 'But if he went to hospital 'tis all tubes and chemicals until past any waking time, all outside nature.'

'He liked hospital,' said Eva, and a tear dropped off the end of her nose (whether it ran down inside or outside she did not know) and landed on her homework.

'He likes home better,' said Mum.

'I'll get a hanky,' said Eva, and went upstairs for one, racing against the coming of tears. Like some desperate last-minute dash to the toilet with the little ones, she thought.

She sat on Gideon's bed for a time. Once again Barbosch, Mooli and Delfont had to be put back there with him. They had no life to give him; Eva had life, but there was no way of giving it.

Gideon asleep, neither taking nor giving, not being in life. Some other world was his, and only Gideon had been there. No one in truth has been to the planet Novendore, but it is there, real enough for the people who live there, though it is only made between the covers of a book.

Gideon between the covers of his own book. Under the covers of his own bed.

His glasses empty on the table beside it, dusk coming through them.

Eva put the landing light on for him: for him, as flowers are for memory.

Mum slept that night, for the most part. Tansy woke everyone at three o'clock because there was a bubble in the room, and finished the night in the bottom bunk with Mercury, untroubled, unbubbled.

In the morning Gideon lying untroubled too, and having stirred the toys to the floor again.

In the afternoon Grandpa Catt and Dad were in Edenfields, still barrowing bricks out of the hearth. Eva stayed there, when Dad said there was no change indoors.

The bricks were warm to the touch, radiating heat. When she touched them they took moisture from her hand, though it was dry, leaving a powder in its place. The powder, she thought, was her own dried self, lying on her own substance.

'A fine hard bake,' said Grandpa Catt, tipping a barrow-load close against the house. 'You can hear them drink the air. Four of these will take a bucket of water and not show it. They're baked like little cakes.'

Eva went to look at the new place formed when they came out of the hearth. Here was a new room, a clay cavern, smelling of oven, of lost heat, of bake.

She planned to live in it.

'Best stay out,' said Grandpa. 'I wouldn't give much for the roof, and when we've emptied it we'll have to pull it down.'

'It's just steady enough to take the bricks out,' said Dad. 'But no more.'

'Come a shower of rain,' said Grandpa, 'and it's own weight will pull it in. It's been here long enough, and there's no more work for it to do.'

Gideon on his bed still sleeping.

Mr Dandow came up into Edenfields and talked to Dad. Grandpa went on wheeling and tipping.

'Either way,' said Dad, at the door to Mr Dandow, at the end of their talk.

'No hurry, Dennis,' said Mr Dandow.

It's the way he thinks, thought Eva; it's not his actual Gideon, and it's all another world.

The smooth-sided head went away, the van slipping into life down the hill.

Gideon still sleeping, Mum in his room.

'They didn't think he was dreaming,' she said. 'It's a harder sleep than that,' and she turned Gideon's head a little, and holding it. 'It never did work very far, since he was ill. And now hardly a thing at all.'

Eva carefully put three soft toys where they now belonged, giving their devotion to Gideon.

The next day was Saturday. Dad and Grandpa Catt were out together very soon, hammering and sawing. Eva had first the management of the little ones, and then went shopping with them and Mum. They came back complete with Mercury, who had attempted to lose a leg in a supermarket trolley, getting it through a microscopic hole. ('Well, I could do with something hilarious,' said Mum. 'No, my lad, you carry it yourself.')

Grandpa was down at the lower end of Edenfields, gathering wood again, bringing it out into the road and walking up the hill with the barrow less full of wood and more full of child than anyone but children wanted. Mercury trying to get his leg through again.

'Thought you'd done that,' said Mum. 'Haven't you done enough?'

'The firing we did,' said Grandpa. 'And enough of that. Next we have to bring down the chimney and the hearth, because they aren't fit to stand, though they do.'

The back of the hearth had been cut away, though not through to daylight, because the back was the base of the chimney. Ten courses of brick had been taken out, the width of a brick at a time, and replaced by upright studs of good timber, the same as that in the roof trusses of the house. Now there was another firing to be done, and as it burnt the support of the chimney would go and the chimney have to fall, bringing the roof of the hearth with it.

'We'll do it as soon as we can,' said Grandpa, as the day went by. Hidden work went on, hidden stocks of wood were placed.

144

'Get it out of the way and done,' said Dad.

'And a few more bricks to be got out afterwards too,' said Grandpa.

Another world, thought Eva. Activities. Gideon would have liked it.

'First we'll know where everybody is,' said Dad, 'and that's indoors. Watch from a top window, if you like.'

'I'll take them in,' said Mum. 'And lock the back door, because I know those two. They'll pretend to be inside, and they might even think they are, and be out there all the time.'

Mercury (limping and lurching like the stricken planet Novendore when the Heliolyser bit the shoulder of it off complete with the Tyrant's headquarters) and Tansy (doing cartwheels without getting her feet off the ground) went indoors and stood on Eva's pillow, to watch from her window.

Eva went in to see Gideon.

Gideon in the middle of his stillness, hair and face showing, nothing more; whole hand and hurt hand under the bedclothes; Gideon as nobody. But Gideon, Gideon, for all that, his dear glasses more like himself than he was; at least letting light through.

Eva, after patting three creatures on their faithful backs, turned her own on Gideon and watched from his window.

Outside there was a sleep too. Something was not quite ready. Dad and Grandpa were standing and talking, and no fire had begun. There was yet no smoke.

Mum came upstairs. Her hand touched Gideon's brow. 'He's cooler,' she said. 'Breathing easier. They talked about hypostatic pneumonia. What's happening out there?'

'They're going in,' said Eva. 'They're there in the dark. They're striking matches. Now they've come out.'

In the next room the little ones sang that they were safe in the arms of Jesus.

Smoke began to falter from the chimney. It became more steady, a dark streak on the darkening sky.

Next door the singing stopped. The little ones went to their own room and began to dress up.

'We'll bath them when the boys outside have stopped playing,' said Mum. 'Because I want to watch.'

It seemed to be a long watch. The dark smoke went away. The cloud of the sky went black enough to disguise it even if it came again. Dad and Grandpa Catt stood off to one side and seemed to be happy about the wait.

Mum turned away from the window and looked at Gideon, where her mind really was.

'If he'd been helping,' she said, 'he'd have wanted another chimney tomorrow. If we could have instant backwards replay during the night, putting it up again.'

'It isn't down yet,' said Eva. 'I think the fire's gone out.'

'Hmn,' said Mum, thinking only of Gideon.

CHAPTER TWENTY

Mum was still looking at Gideon when a visitor came to the door. Eva thought it was Grandpa, coming round that way to tell them everything had failed. The little ones came down with Mum to look.

The visitor was a nurse. 'Doctor asked me to come,' she said to Mum. 'Your boy, isn't it? He has to be turned.'

Turned! thought Eva. What dreadful thing is that?

'Gideon,' said Mum.

The nurse switched her eyes to Eva, having seen her start and stare. 'He mustn't lie in the same position all the time,' she said. 'I'll show you how to turn him,' she continued, quiet and gentle. Mum stopped biting her teeth together and smiled.

147

'I can't tell you anything else,' said the nurse. She knew what she knew, and no more.

'I understand,' said Mum gently back.

The nurse had even charmed Mercury and Tansy. They stood before her with open mouths. They had been eating elderberries, and their mouths had a wild, vivid forwardness. Eva wiped the mouths with a towel, streaking it blue. Saints, she thought. Stains.

'Just the one boy, is it?' asked the nurse. She could make the mistake because Mercury was wearing a dress by now.

'Wearing each other's duds,' said Mum. 'Two of each.'

They had all got upstairs by now. The nurse pulled back Gideon's bedclothes. 'He's only asleep,' she said. 'Gideon. Gideon.'

'He won't hear you,' said Mum. 'He's deaf and retarded, so let him sleep.'

'You don't mean it like that,' said the nurse.

'I mean it,' said Mum. 'But I don't mean I like it.'

'You think you haven't any choice,' said the nurse, camphorating Gideon's shoulder. Eva went to stand by the door, out of the liniment and delicacy.

'I'm used to having no choice,' said Mum. 'You can't choose if there's nothing to choose from. But I know he's made of the same stuff as me. This is my body. And he might not be a big trow, but he's a full one.'

The nurse picked up Paddington and handed him to Eva. 'Barbosch,' said Eva.

From outside in Edenfields there came a shout. It was at the right moment for Eva. She did not wish to see Gideon more uncovered, turned, hauled to another

148

sleeping posture. She picked up Mooli and Delfont, giving one each to the little ones, and went to the window of the room.

There had been a shout, but nothing had changed. The light was the same, early dusk, the fire glittering like the last of the sun. Dad and Grandpa were both there, craning towards the kiln, listening. Eva heard too a cracking of wood, the long splitting of it, more than fire would cause; perhaps what the weight of the chimney would effect.

Slowly, slowly, but more quickly than there was time to see, the chimney knelt, the top half trying to stay upright but carried along by the tumbling foot of its shaft. It came down on itself, and abruptly vanished.

Clouds of smoke and dust had come up in the twilight, making a hole in what could be seen. Novendore's black hole becoming visible. Great sparks, like engulfed suns, flickered. A moment later, and yet in the same moment, the house felt the fall. Downstairs a cup hanging near another rang like a little bell.

In those few seconds the nurse was looking at Gideon's back and elbows. 'What was that?' she asked, unexcitedly but intently.

'My husband and his father demolishing an old chimney,' said Mum. She was splendid and exact, for once, Eva thought. I couldn't have said that.

The nurse was not listening. She had Gideon's hand in hers. 'I saw this in hospital,' she said. 'I thought he was from a home.'

'He is,' said Mum. 'Of a sort.'

'You kept him as long as you could,' said the nurse.

'It looked as if it went into a hole in the ground,' said Eva, turning from the window to report both that fact and that she was there. 'But it was the dust rising.'

'My husband will be in directly,' said Mum. 'Then we can both hear how to do it best.'

Dad rattled at the back door. Eva went down to let him in. Only Grandpa Catt was out of the room now.

'We don't need them all,' said Dad. 'No, I'd best not shake hands. I'm very dirty, and I'll have a swill in a minute.'

The nurse understood that, and then she waited while Dad sent the little ones off to Grandpa Catt outside. 'Quite safe now,' he said. 'I had a quick look round. Have they got to him, Eva?'

'Contact,' said Eva, watching from the window. 'And all the dust has gone and he's got his big torch.'

'You don't need to stay,' said Mum.

'He's my brother,' said Eva. 'I want to know everything.'

'May I have more light?' asked the nurse. Dad turned the switch and the light fell on them all as if it might blister them (like the sun of Novendore).

'Gideon,' said the nurse, 'we're going to turn you over on the other side, dear,' and she straightened his legs. 'He's resting very easy,' she said. 'It's best peaceful.'

'Oh,' said Mum, her hands suddenly trembling, her arms shaking, 'am I doing right? Did I ought to let him go in? Should you take him? Would it be better? I can't ask the doctor, but you're a person, like us.'

'If it's to happen you want to be there,' said the nurse. 'Home is best . . .'

'Dennis,' said Mum, 'are we right?'

'We always said . . .' Dad began, ready to change his mind.

The nurse took Gideon's hurt hand again. Mum took the other, and it trembled with hers.

Gideon feeling something touch him. Gideon sitting up in bed with his nameless shout.

Gideon looking at the nurse, recognizing what she was even without his glasses, grinning, saying, 'Gaboo, gaboo.'

Mum drooped beside the bed, and Dad caught her up. 'Gideon,' she said.

Gideon looking at her.

'Barbosch,' said Eva, squealing, holding Paddington out, not knowing what else there was to do.

Gideon turning his head and looking at her.

'Just asleep,' said the nurse to Mum, quietly.

Gideon saying 'Gaboo' and looking at her.

Then everyone talking at once, Mum standing up on her own, the nurse not knowing who to listen to, Gideon holding Barbosch.

Gideon holding the back of his head. Gideon not holding the back of his head, puzzled.

Gideon waveringly putting his glasses on. Him alive, them alive. Gideon holding the back of his head again.

'Ssh,' said Dad. 'He can hear us. We're making too much noise.'

Gideon getting out of bed, saying 'Deebi', which meant a visit to the bathroom. His foot thudding on the floor so that when he heard it he looked. The floor vibrating like the fall of a distant chimney.

Gideon not being strong enough to walk alone. The nurse thought she could see to all this, but Gideon was not having a Gaboo in the bathroom with him. Dad stepped forward and hoped he was doing the right thing.

Gideon saying 'Dthth' and welcoming the help.

They went out across the landing. Mum sat on the bed, and the nurse suddenly got hold of the back of Mum's neck and pushed her head down between her knees.

'She's a little faintly,' she said. 'Are you right now, my dear?'

'I was all right,' said Mum, sweaty round the mouth. 'The world went black. Am I going to be sick? No, I'm not.'

'No need,' said the nurse, so firm and kind she must be right, and she was. 'You know him so well,' she went on. 'Everything he says sounds the same to me, but you know the different words. You have to know as well as love.'

'We know,' said Mum. 'We love, if love is being turned inside out and torn across.'

In the bathroom the lavatory being flushed. Gideon coming out quickly, holding the back of his head, overwhelmed by a noise he had not expected from outside himself, but comfortable with deebi finished.

Now there were noises from Edenfields. Eva heard them and Gideon seemed to as well. He walked, with Dad's help, across Eva's room, uncertainly locating the distant sounds, and looking from the window towards their source.

The source was the little ones. Gideon not seeing them, but Eva knowing the flash of the big torch. The two of them were coming in with the laps of their skirts full of some heavy material. Grandpa Catt followed, his jacket off and bagged up to hold something.

The nurse sitting with Mum, holding her hand. 'You were doing right,' she said. 'We don't know what is to happen, ever, do we?'

So you don't even know that, thought Eva. Mum's face was watching Gideon.

Gideon watching faces and places, seeing something that no one else saw. Gideon looking for sounds.

There was a tinkling, rattling crash at the back door. 'Bringing in rubbish,' said Eva. 'Must be.'

Gideon hearing language, knowing what it was, wondering what it meant, watching her mouth, checking that words came indeed from there. Gideon saying 'Rauh' but only meaning that he was tired and wanted Dad to take him back to bed.

Gideon comfortable in bed, saying 'Hyagh' and getting Mum's last cold tea to sip at, and saying 'Rauh' again in a more expressive way.

Gideon giving Eva the cup, one arm to Mum, the other to Dad. 'Barbosch,' he said, lying back in his pillows and yawning. Eva gave him Barbosch.

'Gaboo,' he said, and moved his legs.

The nurse obediently pulled his bedclothes over him.

Grandpa came quietly up the stairs. At the bottom of it Mercury and Tansy boiled and bubbled.

'Back, then?' he said, seeing Gideon.

'Bargen,' said Gideon immediately, hearing, repeating,

puzzling, not finding the vision of these sounds useful.

'They've got something,' said Grandpa. 'You've been wanting it, Daph.'

The little ones brought it up in their laps. Grandpa brought some in.

They had found a bright and agreeable plaything, and they knew it was valuable, and they knew it was not theirs. They tipped it out on the bed.

'That's he's,' said Mercury.

'Brown money,' said Tansy.

'In the back of the old chimney, like a place where he put it. I do think they knew,' said Grandpa. 'You heard her come down, old thump shook the ground, lifted the old fowls off their roost next door, old woman come out and cackle too.'

'I thought we might find it some time,' said Mum, and she reached across to tumble the gold and silver coins of Gideon's wages across the counterpane, the thick pounds, the petalled fifties.

Dad went downstairs to answer a knock at the door. He let Mr Dandow in. They stood and talked at the stairfoot for a time, and then came up.

The little ones, having made everybody rich, concluded they had bought the bathroom and retired into it.

Grandpa Catt tidied the money, leaving a grimed grain in the candlewick.

Gideon closing his eyes and falling into a smiling sleep, holding Mum's hand, Eva's.

Mum with tears rolling out of her eyes, not sobbing. 'Don't mind me,' she said to Mr Dandow, when he un-willingly came so far into the house and family.

'Time I went,' said the nurse. 'Most of this I don't understand. But still, I'm glad I came, and I'm glad I'm not wanted any more.'

'You're welcome for yourself,' said Mum.

The nurse saw herself out. Mr Dandow scratched the bristled back of his neck.

'Comed out of it, has he?' he said. 'Right, then Gidden?'

'Righ e idden,' said Gideon, waking a little and going back to sleep.

'Oh, ah,' said Mr Dandow, not knowing how to be polite in sick-rooms. 'Well, Dennis, eh?'

'Well, Daph,' said Dad. 'Eva. Gideon. Dad. What's the noise in there?'

'Nothing,' said Eva, knowing the noise. 'Tansy falling down the toilet.'

'It's all turning normal again,' said Mum. 'Well, did you do it?'

'Yes,' said Mr Dandow. 'We come to an agreement.'

'Yes,' said Dad. 'We fixed it up.' Then he sat and beamed, pleased with what he had done.

'But what is it?' asked Eva. 'What is it, Gideon?' She felt she had better ask someone who did not know, in case she was being too inquisitive.

'Bought the boat,' said Dad. 'Going to be a sailorman on dry land, run the cruises, live at home, me and my crewman, Grandpa tipple out the drinks, up and down the canal, and discos and I don't know what. Bit of both lives, and more regular.'

'Can't be doing with that end of the market,' said Mr Dandow. 'Too old, me and Mrs Dandow. Me, anyhow. So

I'm glad all round, fixing the bargain ('Bargain!' said Dad) and Gidden back in his senses, like you might say.'

'Free trips,' said Eva. 'Is this enough money, that Gideon got?'

In the bathroom rehearsals for the first and last night of Vesuvius went on undisturbed.

Dad rattling the coins on the bed. Gideon opening his eyes.

Gideon saying, hopefully, 'Hoonph.'